LUNA CITY LIMITED

THE PHOENIX AND KATIE LI, BOOK 1

JULIA HUNI

IPH MEDIA

For my friend Tricia,
who even after all these years
supports me one hundred percent.
And roasts awesome coffee.

FOREWORD

This book was first published as an online serial, so it might feel a bit different from my other books. And that's why it has episodes instead of chapters. But it ties in to the *Space Janitor* universe--in fact these characters also play a part in *Waxing the Moon of Lewei*, book three in the *Tales of a Former Space Janitor*.

EPISODE 1: NO MAGIC TONIGHT, YOU PROMISED

THE LITTLE RED shopping cart rumbled across the store, a lopsided wheel vibrating everything inside. Glass clinked against metal as I added another bottle of Three Credit Fred to the basket. Three red, three white, and that case of cheap beer I picked up at Food4Cheap would have to be enough. My wallet wouldn't stretch any farther.

"That register is opening." The voice was deep, with the faintest twinge of a drawl and a subtle rasp that sent a wave of warmth through my body. I turned, and a Hawaiian-shirted Thor smiled at me. Nearly two meters tall, longish blond hair tied back, a faint hint of stubble on his chiseled cheeks. Bright blue eyes and a dimpled smile. This man should be working as a model or actor, not a cashier at the Luna City Milo's Trading Post.

"Thanks." At least I tried to say thanks. My tongue stuck to my teeth, and it came out as an inarticulate mumble. He winked and moved away.

"Damn," I whispered. He must be new—I'd been shopping at that store for months and never seen him before. I'd have to come up with a clever line for the next time he checked me out. Surely, there'd be a next time? I'd been practicing good Karma my whole life—this would be an excellent time for payback.

I waved my NexUs cuff at the check-out screen, and the system registered my account, deducted the amount of the groceries, and sent a receipt to my account. While the bot loaded the groceries into collapsible crates and stacked them in a drone, I peered around the store, trying to locate Thor. No luck. My Ncuff vibrated, and I confirmed the delivery address. With one last hopeful look and several grumpy glares from shoppers trying to get past me to the door, I gave up.

The L train dumped me in the lobby of my apartment building. I took the drop chute to the seventh floor and waved my Ncuff at the door plate. The door slid open.

"Welcome home, Katie. Did you have a good day?"

The house system still gave me the creeps. Its friendly voice and Human-Chat feature were designed to make the user comfortable, but its inability to detect sarcasm reinforced its mechanical nature. I could have set it to use a more robot-like interface—which I infinitely preferred—but Harry liked "Hummy." And the low-end model in our apartment wasn't up to multiple, user-specific personalities.

"Who's coming to the party?" I went into my bedroom and changed clothes while Hummy reeled off a list of names. Half of my office and a bunch of gamer friends of Harry's. Plus a few college friends. I could count on some of them to bring booze and snacks to supplement my meager shopping trip.

"A delivery has arrived," Hummy said. "Shall I open the door?"

"Yes, please." I rolled my eyes at myself. Look at me being polite to the house bot—I refused to call it an AI because it wasn't. Intelligent, that is. Or at least it wasn't self-aware like in a movie. I met the drone in the living room.

The box slid into the room, using mag-lev tech to hover over the rails set in the floor. It stopped about a meter inside. The side wall opened. An arm unfolded from the top, pulled the crates of food and wine from the body of the drone, and deposited them on the floor. Music played, and a voice-over started. "Thank you for shopping at Milo's Trading Post. Please rate your visit on the YesPlease app and earn a code for a free single-serve ice cream. Some restrictions apply."

I lifted one crate and walked through the hologram of dancing dairy desserts to deposit the wine in the kitchen. Nicer places had mag-lev rails all the way to the kitchen, but we had to carry stuff from the door. Not that it was very far. Our "kitchen" was a sink and fridge in one corner of the living room. I stuck the wine into the cooler and retrieved the other crate.

While I unloaded chips and dips onto the counter, the music stopped, and the door opened and closed again. I finished putting away my purchases in blessed silence.

At the bottom of the second crate, I found a box of mints I hadn't bought. Milo's must have a surplus of the things—they'd been hawking them for the last few weeks. Now, apparently, they'd resorted to adding them to unsuspecting shoppers' orders. I tapped my Ncuff and scrolled through the receipt. "They charged me for it! Two credits for a box of mints I didn't want!"

I looked at the ingredients on the tin. Mostly chemicals—no wonder they couldn't sell the things. I stepped into the bedroom and stashed the mints on my dresser. I'd return them Monday—the store wasn't far from my office. And

I'd write a blistering review on YesPlease. Adding unwanted items to a customer's order was not good for business.

"Yo, Katie!" Harry's voice echoed through the tiny apartment.

"Welcome home. How was your day?" Hummy said. According to the specs, the thing didn't differentiate between me and Harry, but it always sounded more sultry when it spoke to him.

"It was a day, Hummy." Harry stuck his head through my bedroom doorway. "You got all the goods?"

"Nice to see you, too. I got beer, wine, food. Do you have the music ready?"

He made finger guns at me. "You know it!"

"No magic tonight, right?" I followed him into the living room. "You promised!"

"But I have a new card trick!" He whipped a deck of cards out of his back pocket and fanned them out. "Pick a card—any card!"

"No." I crossed my arms and shook my head. "No magic. You picked the music, and the menu, and the games. You don't get to do any magic. That was the deal."

"If someone asks—" His smile held hope.

"If someone asks." They wouldn't. At least none of his friends would. And I warned all of mine.

"Rad."

"Where do you get this ancient slang? Been hanging out in the retirement pod?" I started pulling glasses out of the cupboard and arranging them on the tiny counter next to the sink.

Harry worked in the security department at a retirement center. "Those old dudes got it going on." He grabbed a bag of chips and ripped it open with his teeth.

"Did they teach you that, too?" I handed him the scissors. "No teeth—other people are eating those."

He grinned and hacked the ripped edge off the bag. "All hygienic." He dropped the torn scrap into the recycler and tossed the scissors on the coffee table.

"Get to work." I threw another bag of chips at him. "And dump those in a bowl."

He grabbed a bright red plastic bowl off the top shelf and poured the contents of the bag into it. "Right ritzy, we are."

Hummy chimed and announced our first guests. "Citizens Walsh and Zhaeng have arrived."

"Awesome." Harry tapped Hummy's screen and set the door control to open. Then he hooked his audio device to the speaker and music blared. "Let 'em in!"

Our apartment filled rapidly. Friends, neighbors, and coworkers deposited food and beverages on any horizontal surface they could find. The music thumped and people danced.

"How drunk am I?" My best friend, Marjatta, slouched against the wall near the door. "What did you put in that punch?"

"What punch?"

She raised an unsteady hand to point at the coffee table. The chips had disappeared, and the big red bowl now held dark liquid and a few chunks of ice. As we watched, a new arrival dumped the contents of an unlabeled bottle into the bowl, then scooped out a cup and wandered away.

"You might want to avoid the punch." I sipped my second glass of wine. I'd always been a bit of a lightweight, so I had a decent buzz going already. "Have some of Sariah's Skitchy bread. It's to die for." I held out my plate.

Marjatta grabbed a chunk of bread and dipped it into a puddle of dip.

"You might not want to mix those two—"

Too late. She pushed the gooey blob into her mouth and chewed. Within seconds, her eyes bugged out, and her face turned a sickly shade of green. She clamped a hand over her mouth and lunged toward the bathroom.

I bit my lip and shoved the plate into the recycler. As I straightened, I caught a glimpse of Hummy's screen. Harry had overridden the audio notifications, but she still posted guests' names as they arrived. The newest arrival flashed in big letters, filling the screen, then was added to the bottom of a pale gray list in the background. Later, we'd have a record of who attended, in case there were any issues or quarantines.

The newest name was one I didn't recognize. John Smith. An old-fashioned name—something I'd expect to be attached to one of the residents of Harry's old folks' home. I turned to scan the people by the door and spotted him.

Hawaiian Thor.

EPISODE 2: JUST OFF THE BOAT FROM LEWEI

OF COURSE, he wasn't wearing the Hawaiian shirt. A stretchy black T-shirt showed off his broad shoulders and narrow waist. Black pants clung to his legs, and black boots covered his feet. His bright eyes provided a welcome pop of color.

I took three quick steps across the room and stopped in front of him. "What are you doing here?"

"Hey, you're the girl from the store." He smiled, and my brain spun into neutral. "Great party."

"Thanks. You want a drink?" I raised my glass.

"Over there?" He pointed at the kitchen corner. "I'll be right back."

"I can—" He was out of earshot before I could finish the thought. Every head in the room turned as he passed—some curious, most admiring. The girl standing by the drinks smiled and leaned forward, so he could admire her ample cleavage. She said something, her eyelashes fluttering. Thor responded and took the glass she offered. As he turned, he said something else and nodded at me.

The girl glared as Thor returned to my side. The music pounded, and he leaned close to yell in my ear, "I'm John. This your place?"

"Yeah." I nodded my head violently, in case he didn't hear my response. "Me and my roommate, Harry. You know Harry?"

Thor looked around the room, nodding and smiling as he met curious eyes. "That him with the cards?"

Harry offered a fan of cards to the two girls he had pinned in a corner. They

5

each pulled out a card and returned them to the deck without looking at them. Harry didn't seem to notice.

I groaned. "I told him no magic."

"He's not hurting anyone."

"Yeah, but they'll hurt him." One girl said something. The other laughed, and Harry's face fell. The girls pushed past him, giggling.

"See? It happens every time. He never learns."

Harry turned and caught my eye. His face went pink, and he shoved the cards back into his pocket and disappeared into the crowd.

I turn back to John/Thor. "If you don't know Harry, how'd you end up here?"

John shrugged. "Someone mentioned it. Nasir, I think."

"I don't know Nasir." I looked around the room. "Of course, I don't know most of these people."

"Speaking of knowing people, what's your name?" John asked.

I blinked. "Oh, yeah, I'm Katellyn Li. Call me Katie."

"Nice to meet you, Katellyn." His deep, gravelly voice sent warm shivers up my spine.

But the name grated on my nerves. "No. Katie. Please. Only my mother calls me Katellyn."

"I definitely don't want you to associate me with your mother." John smiled, and my toes curled. "You wanna find somewhere quieter?"

"Like where?" I narrowed my eyes at him. I wasn't the type to sneak off with a guy I just met. I watched the news.

He held up both hands. "I'm having trouble thinking with all this noise. And I'd like to get to know you better. I think fate wants us to be… friends. Maybe you have a home office, or a bedroom?" The sexy smile returned.

I crossed my arms.

He grinned sheepishly. "Sorry. I'm coming on too strong, aren't I? Look, I'm new in town, and you seem like you know everyone—I mean, the whole world is here in your apartment. I thought you could help me get to know more people."

"Where are you from?" I settled back against the wall, ignoring his suggestion.

"Just off the boat from Lewei." He said it quietly, as if daring me to make the usual comments about rich boys from Lewei slumming on Luna.

"How was your flight?"

He smiled and leaned against the wall next to me. "Bumpy. Long. Boring."

As we chatted, he fiddled with a heavy, square ring on his right hand. It had a flat face and a small sapphire embedded in the gold. It was an old-fashioned thing, and not something a Leweian would usually waste their travel weight allowance on. Either John Smith was wealthy, or he bought that here.

6

I stopped talking when his attention wandered away from me. I got the impression he was looking for someone. "Are you meeting someone here?"

His eyes snapped to my face. "No. My buddy—Nasir—left a while ago. Another party, I guess. But I thought this one was more interesting."

"How do you know this Nasir? I thought you just arrived—" A noise from the bathroom cut me off. How could I have forgotten Marjatta? "Will you excuse me for a moment?"

"Don't be long."

I rolled my eyes and took the two steps down the hall to the bathroom door. "Marjatta? You okay?"

A groan answered me.

"I'm coming in." I glanced at John Smith as I opened the door. His eyes were fixed on me, watching, calculating. He smiled, and the wary expression disappeared. Or maybe I imagined it.

Marjatta huddled by the toilet. Sweat beaded on her forehead and upper lip, and her hair stuck out in all directions. She wiped her mouth on her sleeve and looked up at me. "What did I do to deserve this?"

"You mixed Sariah's Skitchy bread with Tomi's spicy dip after drinking an unknown mixture of alcohol." I wet a cloth and wiped her face. "Do you want to lie down? You might feel better if you're horizontal."

Her grunt sounded affirmative, so I slid my hands under her armpits and lifted her. Marjatta was born and raised on Luna, so she's tall and thin, with little muscle mass. I moved here as a child and work out daily to keep some semblance of my Leweian strength. After all, I might want to visit someday.

I slid her arm over my shoulders and hustled her out the door. John had disappeared, and an unexpected sense of loss dropped over me. I shook it off— he was hot, but I just met the guy! Marjatta and I stumbled three more steps to my bedroom door, and I waved my Ncuff to it open it.

I locked my bedroom during parties. On Luna, there's no outside, so no need for a place to stash coats. And finding strangers—or friends—hooking up in my bed was not something I enjoyed. The door slid open, and Marjatta lurched to a stop, staring at the Norse god checking the pockets of my discarded dress.

EPISODE 3: DIDN'T THEY TELL YOU LUNITES ARE LIGHTWEIGHTS?

"WHAT ARE YOU DOING IN HERE?" I demanded. "Put my clothes down, you pervert!"

John Smith didn't move. His eyes darted from me to Marjatta, then to the door behind us. Then he smiled. "I found somewhere quiet."

"Save the charm, perv. What are you doing in my room?" I stumbled as Marjatta sagged against me. "Help me get her on the bed."

For whatever reason, I wasn't afraid of him. Having arrived recently from the higher gravity of Lewei, he would be strong enough to overpower both of us—even if Marjatta wasn't drunk. But I didn't get a sense of menace. Just weirdness.

John Smith picked up Marjatta as easily as if she were a child and laid her on the bed. Then he pulled her boots off and set them on the floor.

I dragged a light blanket over her and pointed across the room. "Put that trash can near her, will you?"

John Smith set the plastek cylinder by the head of the bed. "She's out."

"Lunites are lightweights. Didn't they tell you that in your immigration class? Or are you a tourist pretending to be a local?"

"I'm not pretending to be anything." He took a step back, bumping into my dresser. "Sorry." He reached down to steady my lamp.

The movement drew my eyes—something was different. My dresser looked like it always did—a cheap, blocky, plastek box with drawers. The lamp sat on top, with my jewelry box next to it, as usual. That was all.

Then it hit me. The mints I'd found in my Milo's crate were gone. And was

9

that a rectangular box in his pocket? "Did you steal my mints? That's two credits I didn't want to spend, and now you're stealing them?"

"What are you talking about?" He held up both hands. "I didn't take anything."

I pointed. My face went hot as I realized I was pointing at his crotch, but I gritted my teeth. "You work at Milo's Trading Post—buy your own mints!"

His face went blank. "I don't work there—I told you, I just got off the ship from Lewei."

"But you were directing people... Who the hell are you and why are you stealing mints from my locked bedroom?"

Marjatta snored softly, then grunted.

Thor glanced at her. "Is she really asleep?"

I crossed my arms. "Why do you care?"

"Because I shouldn't—look, this is classified, and I shouldn't tell civilians... No."

"Civilians? What are you talking about?"

He seemed to mull something over, then pulled the box of mints from his pocket. "This is a drop—there's a data card." He ripped the clear wrapper off the box and let it fall into the trash. Then he opened the box. A piece of thick paper cushioned the mints. He pulled out the paper and snapped the box closed. "This is what I needed. You can have the mints."

I burst out laughing. "That is the worst story I've ever heard. Admit it, you thought if I found you in my bedroom, I'd let you stay." The words sounded hollow as they left my mouth. I'm moderately attractive, but I'd never inspired a guy to break into my bedroom before. And this guy could have gotten any girl he wanted.

"Ha, you caught me." He closed the distance between us, shoving the paper into his pocket.

I flung up a hand, holding him away. Heat radiated off his chest, warming my icy fingers. "Not so fast. Gimme that."

"This?" He held up the box of mints.

"No, the paper. The data card." I grabbed the box and dropped it on the foot of the bed, then wiggled my fingers in a "gimme" motion.

He froze. "I can't do that."

I studied him. "You're serious. That paper—who are you?"

His eyes flicked to Marjatta again. "Can we go somewhere more private to discuss this?"

"No, we can't. I want to be within earshot of a friendly crowd in case I need to scream."

He chuckled. "They wouldn't hear you over that horrible music."

I bit my lip. He was right. I lifted my chin and faked bravado. "Spill."

He looked around the room, then sighed and perched against the dresser.

"My name is Nick Beckett. I'm an agent with LIA—Lewei Intelligence Agency —code name Lunar Phoenix. As I said, this paper—" He patted his pocket. "— contains a data card I was tasked to retrieve from a source. The drop was at Milo's, but I was being followed. So, I slipped the package into your cart and came here to retrieve it."

I slumped onto the end of the bed. "How did you know where I lived?"

"I could have looked you up in the customer database at Milo's."

"But you didn't."

"It was easier to follow you home."

I leaped to my feet. "You followed me? No way—I would have noticed."

"You didn't. Civilians don't, as a rule."

I shoved a hand through my hair, pushing the thick mass away from my face. "This is—why are you telling me all this? Secret agents don't run around spilling their true identities to *civilians*." I gave the word the same dismissive tone he used.

He nodded. "It's not considered good craft. We have to assume everyone is an enemy agent. But you cornered me, and I needed the drop." He patted his pocket again, then started playing with the ring I'd noticed earlier. "And I have an insurance policy."

"What's that supposed to mean?" Suddenly, I was afraid. This stranger, pretending to be a government agent, could be anyone. I was alone with him— in her drunken state, Marjatta didn't count. The music thumped and wailed outside—a perfect cover for any mayhem he chose to inflict. I took a step toward the door.

He sighed and twisted the face of his ring. The sapphire popped up a few millimeters. "I've enjoyed talking to you—really I have. If the circumstances were different… But I can't risk you remembering any of this."

Breath caught in my throat. "What are you going to do?" My voice came out strangled.

He took my upper arm in one big hand and urged me toward the bed. "You're going to lie down, and I'm going to give you a harmless drug. You'll wake up in the morning and won't remember any of this."

"No! I'll scream!"

He shook his head sadly. "No, you won't. And I promise I won't hurt you." He raised his hand.

I sucked in a deep breath to yell. A cool mist flowed out of the ring, filling my nose and mouth. His face seemed to waver, then slid sideways. My head and body fell against something soft, and my eyes started to close.

He went all wibbly-wobbly as he crossed the room and opened the hazy door. "Sweet dreams, Katie."

The door clicked shut.

Then nothing.

EPISODE 4: PROBABLY BECAUSE YOU DRANK A GALLON OF MYSTERY PUNCH

I WOKE SUDDENLY, like I always do. Out cold one moment, fully awake the next. Something—someone—bumped against my back, and I rolled out of bed before I realized I'd moved.

The lights came up—just enough to light the way to the bathroom. I crouched, staring at the bed. Someone else was there—and I had no memory of who it might be. A quick look down reassured me—I was fully clothed except for my shoes.

The figure in the bed rolled over.

Relief swept through me. Just Marjatta.

Marjatta opened her eyes a fraction of a centimeter. "Wha' time is it?"

"Early. Go back to sleep."

"I feel like crap."

"Probably because you drank a gallon of mystery punch." I looked at my wrinkled clothing again. "I guess I must have, too. Weird. I don't have a hangover."

"Lucky." She groaned and rolled over again. "Where's the guy?"

"What guy?" Panic jolted through me. Had there been a guy? Why didn't I remember?

"The hot one. He was here. Then he left."

"Here—in my room here? Or at the party?"

"I dunno."

"I'll get you some InstaSobr." I padded into the bathroom and opened the cabinet. In the low light, my reflection was hard to see, but I didn't look too bad. "Lights, forty percent."

13

The light grew brighter. I peered in the mirror. My hair was a disaster, and my makeup had smeared, but my eyes were clear. I pulled a packet of anti-intoxicant from the cupboard and took it to Marjatta.

She was snoring, so I left it on the bedside table. After a fast shower, I dressed and went into the living room.

It was trashed, of course. The punch bowl held a puddle of vile-looking liquid and a few empty cans. Popcorn and chips were strewn around the room. Something was smeared across the tiny kitchen floor—I hoped it was one of the bland chocolate cupcakes. A couple of strangers were passed out on the couch, and empty cups covered every surface.

I sent a text to Marjatta and snuck out the door.

I waited for the L train in the building lobby. The air—on "cool morning" setting—felt good against my warm face and arms. Whatever I drank last night hadn't given me a hangover, but it had left me flushed and foggy. The whoosh of moving air heralded the train's arrival, and the doors opened with a waft of heat and grease.

I climbed on, not sure where I was heading. Maybe I'd just ride and try to clear my head. This early on a Saturday, the train was deserted. I zoned out for a few stops, but when the androgynous voice announced Tiergarten Center, I exited impulsively.

Tiergarten is one of the largest domes on Luna. Formal gardens ring the outer edge, and in the middle is a wide, paved expanse. During the day, in the official summer months, several fountains spray water. At night, musicians play—sometimes formal concerts and sometimes random buskers. In the designated winter season, an ice-skating rink covers the plaza.

Of course, summer and winter are fictional on Luna. The moon has a thin, useless atmosphere, so everything is inside controlled-environment domes. But we have seasons matching those on Lewei, synched to the planetary government's capital. The temperature doesn't vary much—just enough to require sweaters in the winter. It was late spring now, and the flowers were blooming in Tiergarten.

I wandered aimlessly across the dome. A few other early risers passed—walking or jogging. I stopped to get coffee at a food cart, then headed through the west tunnel into the Hills.

The Hills were a series of interlocked domes with rolling green fields and transparent hulls that allowed visitors to see the stars and planet. They were frequently used for therapy sessions for homesick newcomers, but even long-timers enjoyed the cool grass. When I was a kid, I used to roll down these grassy slopes.

I climbed over the first low rise and settled on a bench to enjoy my coffee. A flock of projected birds swirled overhead, chirping. Nearby, a frog croaked—or a recording of a frog croaked.

I'd just about finished my cup when a voice caught my attention—someone was whispering nearby. The green dunes and the low ceiling of the Hills combined to create some odd acoustical effects. The men might be three or four rises away, but I could hear them clearly.

"—isn't the right one."

"It's the one that was dropped." A second voice, deep with a faint, sexy rasp, like running my hand across velvet. "This isn't my first pickup. I got the right one."

"Then the girl must have taken it. Who is she with?" the higher, lighter voice answered.

"She's a civilian. The wrapper was intact when I retrieved it. Something else is going on." This voice made me want to melt. I'd always had a soft spot for a Southern Leweian drawl. And I had the nagging conviction I should know the owner.

I stood. I'd grown up in Luna City. My friends and I had played Marco Polo in these Hills. Tracking down the whisperers was a game we'd loved. With a devious grin, I tossed my empty cup into the recycler and stalked my prey.

At the top of the next rise, I lost the conversation—as I expected. The little valley between this hill and the next was empty, so they were to the west. I walked along the narrow path winding between the dunes, stopping at strategic intervals to listen.

The pavement curved around the next dune, and I'd have bet my lunch credits my quarry would be there. I wiped the grin off my face and sauntered around the corner.

Two men looked up. The shorter one nodded. "No problem. It's easy to get turned around in here."

I suppressed my smile. That was the higher-voiced man. Which meant the tall, muscular one was my southern-voiced stranger.

The shorter man raised a hand and hurried away.

"Good morning." The big guy gave me a pleasant smile.

"I guess your friend is in a hurry." I looked him over. "Do I know you? I think we've met before."

"Not likely. I just landed yesterday."

"And got lost in the Hills first thing." I pointed at the dome where the transparent overhead met the solid sides. "You can always find the exit—look for the little green arrows. It's a required safety feature."

"I wasn't sure it was okay to walk on the grass." We started up the dune, following the green arrows.

"That's what it's here for. I'm sure I've met you." I snapped my fingers. "You were at Trader Milo's. I thought you were one of the employees."

He laughed easily. "I won't make the mistake of wearing a flowered shirt in there again. Three people asked me to help them find something called Siena Chips."

"Yeah, they discontinued those a few weeks ago." We reached the top of the dune. "See—the entrance is there. Incidentally, you should be careful about secret meetings in the hills—sound carries."

His face went blank. "Secret meetings?"

"Yeah, you said something about picking up a girl. And a—" I broke off as a series of scenes—memories?—passed through my head. This man in my apartment, getting a drink. In my room, holding a box of mints. Leaning against my dresser, talking about data cards and civilians.

The ground seemed to tilt. I reached out blindly for anything to keep my balance. A warm hand gripped mine, solid as the stone of Luna. I looked at his fingers, holding mine, and a square gold ring with a sapphire. I jerked away in fear.

"You. You were in my apartment. You drugged me."

EPISODE 5: NO ONE INVITES A STRANGER FOR A CUP OF OJ

"JOHN—NO, Phoenix? Wait, I got it. Nick. Nick Beckett. Leweian—" I took a half-step forward and lowered my voice. "LIA?"

Nick Beckett's face remained blank, but his left hand played with the ring on his right. "I don't know what you're talking about."

"Drop it." I pointed at the ring. "You know exactly what I'm talking about. And if you don't want half of Luna City to know, you'll admit it, and we can go somewhere less public."

He reached for me. "I think you're unwell. I'll escort you to a medical center. Where is it?"

I stepped back. "Not a chance." I turned and jumped.

In Luna City, with our low gravity, leaping is a more efficient way to move quickly than running. Long jumps with a low arc let us cover distance at an astonishing rate. Planet-dwellers—like Nick Beckett—might be stronger, but they have to learn the Luna Leap.

In three long jumps, I reached the top of the next dune. I timed my jumps perfectly, picking up speed and distance with each leap. Four more brought me within sight of the dome hatch. Normally, it would be clear at this time of day —early on a Saturday. But today, my luck was out. A huge group of Leweian tourists—obvious in their strange dirt-side clothing—followed a guide carrying a tall pole with a sign on top.

I stutter-jumped—shifting my leap more vertical to bleed off speed, then rolled into the padded wall beside the hatch—placed there for the exact purpose I had just demonstrated. With a "Ta dah!" I jumped to my feet, then melted into the crowd.

Or tried to. A hand closed around my wrist. Big, warm, with a sapphire ring.

Crap.

"Let go of my arm, or I'll scream." I tried to keep my tone conversational, but it came out with a hysterical edge.

"Please." He ushered me out of the crowd and into the Hub. This was a smaller dome connected to the Hills and the rest of Luna City via trains and underground tunnels. His voice sounded almost panicked. "Let me buy you a coffee, and we can talk. Any restaurant you like."

"Any restaurant?" I smirked. I'd always wanted to go to Reanta's but couldn't afford the water, much less the coffee. "I know just the place. I hope you get a good per diem rate."

Why did I agree to go with him? I still didn't get any hint of menace from him. I had a pretty good sense of self-preservation, and my gut was telling me this guy wasn't a threat. Probably a stupid assumption to make about an LIA operative, but I never said I was smart.

We took the drop chute down one floor and angled across the hub toward the BH connector. We could have taken the subway, but I wanted witnesses if anything happened. The train stations could be empty this early, but the tunnels always had occupants.

Small tents stood along the walls of the tunnel between the Hub and Beijing Dome. Luna City was overcrowded and overpriced. Those who couldn't afford rent lived in tents in the tunnels. The place was clean—the local police saw to that. Anyone who left debris outside their tent was deported to Lewei where they'd likely end up in a debtors' prison or work camp. Or a morgue if they couldn't take the gravity.

Nick Beckett expressed no surprise at the row of makeshift shelters. Most tourists were encouraged to avoid the tunnels, but either he'd been down here before, or he'd been warned.

Faces peered at us from beneath the shadowed openings. I stopped at a striped tent about two-thirds of the way to Beijing and dropped a Lunatic—the small paste-board coins used for under the table transactions—into the cup sitting at the entrance. "Good morning, Mother Frane."

A wrinkled face smiled up at me. "Good morning, Katie. How are you today?"

"I'm good. Are you getting enough to eat?"

She patted her thin stomach. "Plenty enough, thanks to you and others like you."

"I'll stop by to chat later—I have a business meeting." I cast a narrow look at Nick, then leaned forward conspiratorially. "Can't leave the Lewei bigwigs waiting."

Mother Frane sized Nick up. Her smile faded, and she looked him over a second time. "Be careful with this one. I sense danger."

I looked from the old woman to Nick. I usually laughed at Mother Frane's predictions and pronouncements, but sometimes she was right. Based on my recently returned memories, this might be one of those times, even if I didn't feel it myself. "I'll be careful. That's why I stopped by. Witnesses."

She grinned and pointed a crooked finger at Nick. "Got you in my data bank." She tapped her temple. "Don't mess with Katie."

"I wouldn't dream of it." Nick dropped a paper credit note into the cup with a smile.

Mother pulled the five-credit note out, her eyes widening. "Don't think you can buy me off, neither."

He bowed respectfully and gestured for me to continue. I squeezed the old woman's hand and turned away.

The hatch to Beijing Dome was huge—four meters high and twice as wide. Meter-thick doors hid in the side walls. If the dome or the tunnel lost pressure, the doors automatically slammed into place at each entrance. Additional doors blocked the tunnel at the midpoint. I'd never seen or heard of it happening in my eighteen years in Luna City.

The tunnel led into a light industry zone—small family-run businesses. On a Saturday morning, most of them were open and operating—art studios, bakeries, manufacturing unique to Luna City. We passed a martial arts gym, an ice creamery, and a coffee roaster.

"Is that where we're going?" Nick paused to suck in a deep breath of the coffee-scented air.

"No, they're a wholesaler. We're going up to Reanta's on the fourth floor."

"That sounds familiar."

"It's on the tourism bureau's 'not to be missed' list." I thought I'd heard that somewhere, but it wasn't something a local would know.

We walked through another arch into the center of the enormous dome. Beijing was taller than Tiergarten but circular rather than ovoid. The middle of the dome featured an open well that stretched from the curved ceiling to the bottom floor, many levels below the moon's surface. Balconies ringed each floor, with six drop chutes evenly spaced around the circle.

We took a chute up to the fourth floor and found seats at the café. Tables and chairs filled the open space between the central well and the shop—there were no seats "inside" since the entire dome was inside. It was relatively empty because we'd arrived well before the fashionable hour. We took a two-seat table against the railing. White tablecloths covered the tables, and the menu glowed through the fabric.

"Their specialty is beignets." I tapped the menu and flipped to the pastry section. "I suggest we get a basket."

He waved expansively, like a genie granting wishes. "Choose whatever you like."

"The LIA must pay well." I tapped the image of their largest basket and added a café au lait for myself. "What are you drinking?"

"Black coffee." He tapped his Ncuff against the table, authorizing the payment, and the menu faded.

We people-watched for a while. At least, I watched the people—and him. I wasn't sure what he was doing. His eyes drifted over the shops on the floors above and below us, returning to my face from time to time. His expression was neutral, with a small quirk to his lips, as if I amused him.

He caught me staring and smiled. I looked away, my cheeks hot. Why was I embarrassed? This guy had used false pretenses to get into my home, broken into my room, stolen my mints, then drugged me.

There's a sentence I never thought I'd say.

Why was I having coffee with him? I should have turned him over to the authorities. He could just wave his LIA credentials and get out jail free, right?

A server—a human server, not a bot—brought our coffee. "The beignets will be out in a moment." He set the cups in front of us and disappeared through a dark door.

I sipped my drink and looked Nick up and down. "Right, let's get down to business. What's an LIA operative doing in Luna City?"

He set his coffee on the table, untasted. "Let's call it 'the company,' shall we? What were you saying about the sound traveling in that park?"

I tried to remember what he was talking about—the returning memories had mixed in with the events of the morning. "Oh. The Hills have weird acoustics. I could hear you talking about—I guess you were talking about me." My eyes narrowed. "Doesn't that seem a little coincidental?"

"It does, indeed. Who do you work for?"

"Luna City, LTD."

He lifted his cup again. "Not your cover job. Which organization are you with? GIA? LLE? You're not a Commonwealth operative, are you?"

The waiter returned with a basket of hot, pillowy pastries. He used silver tongs to put one on each plate, then sifted powdered sugar over them. With a flourish, he produced two forks and placed them on the table. "Bon appétit."

I leaned forward and breathed in the sugary, fried goodness. Then I remembered to be insulted by his comment. "I am not a Colonial agent. I am a loyal Leweian and a customer service agent for Luna City, LTD."

"What's that, a tourism thing?" He picked up the fork and stabbed the pastry, releasing a waft of steam.

"No, we're a novelty company." I picked up the beignet and bit into it with a sigh. He could cast all kinds of unpatriotic aspersions if he bought me beignets.

20

"A what?" He poked the beignet again.

"Stop that. Just eat it. You won't be sorry." I lifted my cup for a sip. "We're a novelty company. We sell lunar novelties. You know, anti-gravity shoes, dehydrated ice cream bars, miniature moon habitats."

He set the fork down. "Luna City, LTD? The place that advertises zero-gravity whoopee cushions?"

My face heated. "Yes."

"And you don't work for a covert government agency?"

"Of course not. Although, now that I think about it, my job would be an excellent cover. I talk to people all over the system. And ship stuff to them. You need any messages passed? Maybe I should apply. Is 'the company' hiring?" I made air quotes around the phrase.

He cocked his head at me. "I almost believe you."

"Why wouldn't you?"

"Too many coincidences. Why were you at Milo's yesterday?" He picked up the coffee again.

"Shopping. For the party." I used my best "duh" voice. "Why were you there?"

"I told you. But why were you in the Hills this morning—who tipped you off?"

"No one. I go there when I want some space. And when I want to hide from my roommate. Did you see our apartment? It's a disaster. If I stay away long enough, he'll clean it. If I go home, he'll give me those sad puppy dog eyes and expect me to help him."

"Isn't cleaning up afterward part of the deal with parties?" He set his coffee down, untasted, for the third time.

"We had a deal." I pointed my fork at him. "If I invited my friends, he would do the cleanup. But if I go home…" I shook my head and ate the last bite. "Why aren't you drinking your coffee?"

"I was waiting to see if it was poisoned."

My mouth dropped open.

He laughed and picked up the cup. "Just kidding. I don't actually like coffee. But no one invites a stranger out for a cup of orange juice."

"Ah." I nodded wisely. "It's part of your cover."

"Exactly. Are you done?" He gestured to the table.

"Only if I can take the rest of those home." I tapped the silver basket holding the remaining four pastries.

"Of course." He signaled to the server. "Add another order to go."

The waiter carried the beignets away and returned with a huge HotKrisp bag, which he presented to me with a flourish. Nick dropped a handful of Lunatics in the man's subtly extended hand, and we departed.

"I'll walk you home."

"Why?" I looked around the atrium as we strolled toward the drop chute. "So you can drug me again?"

Nick's steps faltered.

I stopped and swung around on him. "Were you planning on drugging me again?"

"If I say no, will you stop attracting so much attention?"

"Only if it's true." I glared.

He stared back, face blank. I was coming to recognize that as his plotting face.

"What are you up to?" I took a step backward.

"Nothing." He held out a hand. "Truce?

EPISODE 6: I'M NOT SURE 'BENEFITRIX' IS A REAL WORD

"TRUCE? WHY SHOULD I TRUST YOU?" I stopped in the middle of the atrium, blocking traffic to the drop chute. People ignored us, swarming around on either side. But if I screamed, I'd have hundreds of witnesses.

His hand dropped, and he stepped closer. "You have my word I won't hurt you."

My eyes narrowed.

He heaved a sigh. "Or drug you. I need to look at that mint tin. As you heard in the Hills, I didn't get what I was looking for. It must have been inside the tin rather than the paper."

I checked my Ncuff. Harry was home, and according to Hummy, two visitors were still there as well. I tapped the voice-to-text button. "Did they clean up?"

"The contents of the apartment have not been moved since your departure." Hummy sounded mildly reproving—as if this were my fault. I tapped the disconnect.

"I'll get the tin. You will wait in the lobby." I swiveled on my heel and stalked around him to the drop chute.

We took the L train to my building's lobby. Luna's residence blocks were built down into the lunar soil. A solid dome protected us from the lack of breathable atmosphere and solar radiation. Trains ran between the residence blocks and the common areas in the domes. There were access tunnels to the blocks, too—like the one we took between the Hub and Beijing—except they were deep underground, narrow, and poorly lit, with no friendly homeless people to provide safety. No way I was taking this guy through the tunnels.

The train slid through the atmospheric force shield covering the entrance to the dome and stopped. An articulated collar extended from the lobby doors and latched onto the train. Blowers hummed, pushing air into the space between the two sets of doors. Once the pressure had been equalized, the doors slid open.

We stepped into the lobby—an oblong dome built above the residence block. It was about ten meters wide and fifty meters long, providing enough room for a train car full of passengers to wait.

I poked Nick Beckett in the chest. "You wait here." I crossed the cold, echoing room to the drop chutes on the far wall and waved my Ncuff at the access panel. The door slid aside, and I dropped to the seventh floor.

Our apartment was the third on the left. The door stood open, and loud music filled the hallway.

"Hummy, turn the music down fifty percent." I shut the door behind me.

"Hey, we're listening to that. And we need the fresh air." Harry stood in the middle of the living room with a large recycling bin in one hand and a plate of half-eaten food in the other. The two friends who had crashed on the sofa the previous night stood in the corner rinsing bottles and shoving them into the recycler.

"Opening the door to get fresh air is ridiculous," I said. "If you want people to know you're from the dirt, that's a great way to do it." I held up the HotKrisp packet. "You guys want some breakfast?"

"Where'd you get those?" The greasy-looking blond lunged across the room at the word breakfast.

"I met a friend for coffee."

Blondie had the bag open and breathed in deeply. "Yeah, but these look like the beignets from Reanta's. How can you afford them?"

The bald guy smacked his friend's arm and grabbed a pastry. "Dude. Use your adult manners. You don't ask people how much they make."

"I didn't." Blondie shoved half a beignet into his mouth and spoke around the food. "I just said —"

"Don't say it." The bald dude made a half bow in my direction, swirling his hands in a complex pattern. "Thank you, O kind benefitrix, for this glorious repast."

I tried not to roll my eyes—Harry's friends were such nerds. "I'm not sure 'benefitrix' is a real word, but you're welcome. How do you know what the beignets as Reanta's look like?"

Blondie grinned. "I worked there for a few weeks last year. But they wanted me to be all professional and crap."

Bald guy took another pastry. "You mean they expected you to come to work on time?"

I snickered. "I gotta get something and run." I hurried into the bedroom.

Marjatta was still passed out on the bed, the InstaSobr untouched on the bedside table.

I looked around the room. Where had the mint tin ended up? My memories of last night got fuzzy toward the end. I remembered talking to Nick here in the bedroom. He'd taken the little paper out of the tin and stuck in his pocket, but then what? Did he take the box, too? If he had, he wouldn't have sent me down here to get it, right?

Or maybe he was just trying to get rid of me? No, he seemed worried—panicked even. And if he wanted to get rid of me, he could've simply let me walk away.

As if summoned by my thoughts, I heard his drawl. "—looking for Katie."

"She's in there," Harry's bald friend said.

I swung around as Nick walked into the bedroom and shut the door. "What are you doing in here? I told you to wait upstairs. And how did you get down here? Only residents should be able to get in."

He shrugged. "I stepped into the drop chute and came down. Just like last night."

I tapped my Ncuff. "But last night, we set the access code to allow visitors. I made sure it was restricted again when I woke up this morning. And your name isn't showing up." I waved my NexUs cuff in front of his face. "How did you do that?"

He didn't answer my question. "Did you find the mints?"

"You had them last. Where did you put them?"

"I thought I gave them to you."

"Right before you drugged me? I probably dropped them." I got onto my knees and peered under the bed. Nothing.

"Here they are." His voice sounded subdued.

I stood. Nick held the open tin in his hand, a sheen of sweat making his face glow.

"What's wrong?"

"It was on the table. Open." He poked his finger into the tin, stirring the little white discs around. "There's no chip. But some of the mints are missing. What if the chip wasn't in the paper but was inside a mint?"

EPISODE 7: TAKE THAT TO YOUR SECRET LABORATORY

"DON'T you have some way to identify it? Like a chip scanner or something?"

"You've been watching too many videos." He snapped the tin shut and shoved it in his pocket. "I should have taken this with me last night. Can't believe I'm screwing up my first mission."

"Your first mission? You mean you've never done this before?" The fear factor dropped significantly. The idea of interfering with an official LIA investigation had terrified me. That faceless agency was much scarier than Hawaiian Thor. But if this guy was just a beginner, then he was in way more trouble than me.

He got down on his hands and knees to look under the bed. "It's not my first, first mission. But it's my first mission on Luna. It was supposed to be easy. Walk in, buy the mints, take the shuttle back to Lewei." He slammed his hand against the floor. Then he looked at Marjatta in surprise. "She sleeps like the dead."

"You didn't see how much of that punch she drank. You don't suppose she swallowed your precious chip, do you? Will it hurt her?"

"It's not dangerous. It's just a data chip. But I need to get it." He eyed Marjatta as if she were a giant mint tin to be opened.

I went cold. Ignoring my fear, I pushed between the man and my friend lying comatose on the bed. "I won't let you touch her."

He waved a hand. "Don't worry, I'm not going to cut it out of her or anything. In fact, if she swallowed it, I'm out of luck. I don't think it would survive the trip through."

"Maybe it's still in the box. You can take that to your secret laboratory and check, right?"

He barked out a laugh. "My secret laboratory. Right. I have a scanner in my hotel room."

"I thought you said a scanner was science fiction."

"No, I said you watch too many vids." He looked around the room as if at a loss for words. "Thanks for your help. I should go."

"Are you leaving Luna City?" I bit my tongue as soon as the words came out of my mouth. I didn't care where Nick Beckett was going. I didn't want to get involved with the LIA. Although the idea of never hearing his velvet voice again made me sad. "Never mind. Good luck. Don't let the door hit you on your way out."

I picked up the packet of InstaSobr and popped a tablet into my hand. "Time to get Marjatta sobered up." When Nick didn't respond, I turned, but he was gone.

––––––––

The boys had saved a single beignet, probably because they couldn't shove any more food into their stomachs. Or maybe to leave room for the pizza Harry had promised in exchange for their help cleaning up. After they left, I got some InstaSobr into Marjatta. Predictably, she was starving, so I gave her the left-over pastry and a vat-meat sandwich.

Vat-meat was the meat substitute grown on Luna. Thinly sliced, it resembled deli meat. Or so I was told. Having grown up in Luna City, I hadn't eaten real deli meat since I was four. All I knew was if you put enough mustard on it, it was quite edible.

"Did you find your mystery man?" Marjatta asked around a bite of sandwich.

I choked on my fizzy water. "Mystery man? Who do you mean?"

"The hot guy you were talking about this morning." She chugged half a liter of fizzy water and shoved more sandwich into her mouth.

I wracked my brains, trying to remember what I might have said. "*You* said something about a mystery man. *I* think he was a hallucination."

"Then where'd you get this?" She waved the HotKrisp wrapper. "I've made it my mission to try every pastry in the city. This tastes like it came from one of the high-end bakeries. I suppose it could be homemade—highly unlikely, given the wrapper—or it's from one of the places you can't afford. Which means a guy."

I hunched a shoulder. "Maybe it was a girl. Or maybe I just treated myself."

She stacked the wrapper on top of her plate and laughed. "You? Treat yourself? You are the cheapest woman I've ever met. And sure, it could be a girl, but you're into dudes, so I'm betting it was a guy."

I relented. "Fine. It was a guy I met last night. He took me out for coffee, but he wasn't nearly as much fun sober. Nothing more to say."

"You are cold. Give the guy another chance. Even with InstaSobr, he might have a hangover. You gotta make allowances for that. Plus, he bought you expensive pastries."

"No, he's going back to Lewei."

"Ooh, a planet man. You know they have bigger muscles—and I mean *all* their muscles." She waggled her eyebrows.

"I'm not looking for muscles right now."

"What are you looking for? You're twenty-two years old—the prime of your life. You should be goofing off, playing the field, enjoying yourself."

"That's easy for you to say—you have a trust fund."

"Yeah, I get an allowance—but it's not that many more credits than you make. But that's what I'm saying. You don't need to have credits—you're a pretty girl. Make friends with the planet guy—if he can afford to come here, he's got credits to burn. And he'd love to burn them on you."

"He's here on business." I picked up the plate and wrapper and took them to the kitchen.

"Even better—that means he'll be back."

I thought about Nick's face when he realized he'd blown his mission. "Maybe not."

Marjatta stood. "I gotta head home. There's a thing tonight at the Varian Center. You wanna come? It's a gala for some random lunar dignitary. Mom says I have to go." She pulled her Ncuff out of her pocket. A handful of something white came with it, hitting the table with a faint tinkle. "Oh, sorry." She strapped the device onto her wrist.

I looked at the crumbled white things, my stomach sinking. "What is that?"

"Some mints I found in your room. They were vile. Look, this one has something in it. You should file a complaint against the company!" She scooped the remains of the mints into her palm and held them out to me.

I dropped the plate on the counter and put out my hand. She dumped a pile of crumbled disks into it. A piece of black plastek lay amid the ruins.

"Seriously, you got the receipt? Sue their asses. Then you'll have plenty of credits to party with me." She dusted her hands on her pants, leaned forward to kiss my cheek, and sauntered out the door.

After it closed, I lifted the tiny strip of black with my fingernails. The rest of the mint crumbled away, leaving me in possession of what had to be Nick's secret chip.

EPISODE 8: YOU'RE STALKING THAT DUDE?

I STARED at the chip in my palm. How the heck was I going to find Nick Beckett? He'd never mentioned what hotel he was staying in. Or what name he had checked in under. Nick Beckett was almost certainly another alias, but was it the one he used here on Luna?

I ripped the cleanest corner from the HotKrisp wrapper, folded it around the piece of plastek, and tucked it into my pocket. That should keep me from losing it. But now what?

Absently, I smoothed the thick paper, tracing the logo imprinted on it. I could go back to the café and see if they would tell me anything. Or I could try Milo's. He might have gone back to look for the chip in another tin. How had he identified this one? Did he use that scanner he mentioned?

I slid the plate into the sink and folded the rest of the beignet wrapper to put into the recycler. Printed text caught my eye. I smoothed the paper again, tipping it to catch the simulated sunlight from our virtual window.

It was a receipt, printed on the paper. The total made my eyes water. That much for two coffees and a basket of fried dough? The beignets were good, but were they that good? Only if someone else was paying.

Then the last line of the receipt registered in my sluggish brain: XXXXXXX2345 John Smith.

He'd paid with his Ncuff. John Smith must be the identity he was using on Luna. All I had to do was find a hotel with a John Smith registered. That shouldn't be too hard. An old-fashioned name like that would be unique and memorable. But where to start?

I tore the receipt free and threw the remaining wrapper into the recycler.

Maybe Harry or one of his friends could find him. Harry knew some sketchy characters—hacking hotel databases would be right up their alley. Or running a facial recognition program on the lunar security system. I tapped my Ncuff and buzzed him.

"Yo, Katie, what's up?" I couldn't tell from the vid where he was, but it was dark and noisy.

I explained what I wanted.

"You're stalking that dude?" Harry laughed and ripped off a huge chunk of pizza with his teeth. He chewed, then spoke around the mouthful. "Didn't he give you his contact info? If he didn't, drop it. He's not that into you."

My face heated. "He left something here, and I wanted to return it. Can't you use your hacker skills to track him down?"

Harry's head shook. "You've been watching too many vids. None of that stuff is real. I mean, I could find him if he was at the Happy Skies, but I don't have access to the rest of the city's surveillance systems."

"I doubt he's at your retirement village." I sighed. "Thanks for your help."

"Why don't you try the shuttle port? He's flying back to Lewei today."

"How do you know that?"

"You gotta learn to listen." He pointed his crust at me. "He said he was leaving today. He probably *did* give you his contact info, but you weren't paying attention."

"Believe me, I was paying attention. But that's a great idea. Thanks. Gotta go." I tapped the screen and cut him off mid-word.

Patting my pocket to make sure the chip was still there, I shoved the receipt into another pocket, just in case, and headed out the door.

———

I transferred from the L train to the S and settled down for the long ride. The S train ran from the Luna City hub to the shuttle port, situated fifty kilometers from town. The lunar domes were almost indestructible, but keeping rocket-firing spacecraft away from people's homes seemed like a no-brainer.

Not to mention the single point of entry allowed the government to keep strict tabs on who arrived and departed.

The train slid out of the tunnel under Luna City and zipped across the barren landscape. After we passed the air processing plants and mineral smelters, the red-gray surface of the moon stretched to the horizon, marked by the occasional impact crater.

This train was a two-car model, and each self-contained module held thirty seats. Mine was nearly empty. They ran on an automated schedule, whether they were full or empty. I settled back in my seat and played with an app on my Ncuff. I'd make John Smith reimburse me for this trip—the ticket price would bite into my entertainment budget for the next month if he didn't.

Forty minutes later, I peered out the window as the train curved to the north to enter the terminal tunnel. Trains from other settlements on Luna used the same entrance, so we had to wait our turn. My car rattled as a shuttle blasted away from the launch pad, the thin atmosphere of the moon barely transmitting the sound.

I hoped Nick wasn't on that shuttle.

After an interminable wait, another two-pod train shot out of the tunnel, and we eased in. We slid along the dark passage for several minutes, then eased to a halt. The safety hatch shut behind us, and airlocks sealed around the doors. With a hiss, the automated doors slid open.

I stepped into the gray-tiled terminal. I'd been here before, of course, when greeting high-profile clients for my company. Usually, that was well above my pay grade, but when the PR staff went on holiday, they recruited some of the higher earning call center girls to help. I'd also come here with my parents on the rare occasions my grandparents visited from Lewei.

Signs embedded in the tile walls led to the arrival and departure lounges. Having never flown off-world, I hadn't been to the departure lounge before. I took a deep breath to settle my stomach and slowed my pace to a brisk walk. I didn't want to draw attention. When handing a secret chip off to a fellow spy, one should strive to be cool.

A couple with a small child pushed past me, jumping almost as fast as I'd gone in the Hills. Maybe they were late for their shuttle. Then a pair of young women leaped past. I looked over my shoulder. Another train must have arrived at the station. Dozens of people hurried along the corridor, the Lunites leaping smoothly along the passage, the Leweian tourists easy to pick out from their clumsy movements.

Maybe being cool would draw more attention than hurrying. I pushed off in a short leap and followed the throng up the ramp.

Our progress slowed, then halted as we piled up against a checkpoint. I gulped. Were they checking IDs? Would they want to know where I was going and why? I had no plausible excuse for leaving Luna.

Sweat broke out on my forehead, and my light clothing felt heavy and hot. The crowd in front of me pushed, forming a scrum in front of a narrow doorway. I glanced over my shoulder. Maybe I should go back to the train. John Smith was a trained agent—he could fend for himself. He didn't need an amateur like me drawing attention to his mission. I could drop the chip into a recycler and go home.

I turned, but the people behind pushed me forward. The smell of so many bodies crushed together burned my nose. Or maybe that was my own fear. I tipped my head toward my shoulder and took an experimental sniff. Nope, not me, thank the stars.

Faster than I expected, the crowd ahead of me thinned, and I found myself face to face with a man in a severe black uniform. Heavy gold braid hung from his left shoulder, and shiny silver buttons paraded down the center of his chest. He stood at attention beside a tall counter, his white gloved hand holding a baton across the door to the departure lounge.

The man raised his baton in salute, and the couple waiting stepped through. "Next!" The baton snapped across the entrance.

The crowd pushed me forward. I clenched my teeth and breathed in through my nose, trying to stifle my fear. "Hi. I'm not sure—"

He looked me over. Then his eyes snapped to the far wall. "Do you have travel insurance?"

I froze. "I—no."

"Would you like to buy some?"

"No?"

"Very well." The baton snapped up. "Next!"

"That's all?"

"Next!"

The man behind me muttered something under his breath about stupid tourists. I bit back a retort and hurried through the doorway.

The departure lounge was a huge, circular room. Large screens filled the walls, showing a life-sized view of the launch pad and ugly lunar landscape. If you ignored the occasional pixilation, it almost looked like floor-to-ceiling windows. I turned. The wall by the entrance showed safety videos and documentaries about Luna. I'd seen most of them in school, but the one about the construction of Shinzen City looked new.

I shook myself. *Focus, Katie, you need to find John Smith and get rid of this chip!*

I strolled through the crowd, casually glancing at the other passengers. The families returning from vacation were easy to spot by their colorful clothing and whiny children. A couple with a small baby had more luggage than seemed practical—perhaps they were moving to the surface. Most of the other passengers wore business attire and carried briefcases or messenger bags. They sat absorbed in their computer screens or NexUs cuffs. One of them glanced at me as I passed. His eyes traveled over me, settling on my empty hands.

I hurried away before we made eye contact, cursing my stupidity. My total lack of baggage made me stand out. I was not cut out for this secret agent business. I needed to find John Smith and hand off the chip.

As if summoned by my thought, a tall, broad-shouldered man rose and crossed to the beverage vendor. Nick Beckett.

Funny how I could think of him as John Smith in the abstract, but as soon as I saw him, the other name felt so much more appropriate. He was definitely a Nick. Or maybe Thor.

He finished filling his bottle and turned.

I tried to smile, but it came out as a sickly grin.

Nick looked around casually, then sauntered toward the restrooms.

Did he want me to follow him? I wandered a few steps in the direction I'd been going, then curved around to the left and approached the facilities from the other side. He disappeared through a door marked "family." I hesitated, cast a quick look around to make sure no one was watching, and reached for the knob. The door opened, and I stepped inside.

"What are you doing here?" The words, low and quick, burst out of him almost before the door closed. He snapped the lock shut.

We stood in a small, white-tiled room. Two toilets, one standard and one tiny, stood side by side in the corner. Two sinks, one with a step beneath it, hung from one wall, and a baby changing station, complete with diaper vendo, took up the opposite one.

"Nice meeting place." I shoved my hand into my pocket and pulled out the torn wrapper.

"I had to improvise. Why are you here?" Nick pinned his brilliant blue gaze on me.

I handed him the paper. "I found this."

He looked at it, then waved it at me. "This isn't my real name, if that's what you're worried about. No one can trace this purchase to me."

"What?" I stared at the receipt. "No—sorry, that's not—" I pulled the folded paper from my other pocket and unfolded it. "I found this."

His sharp intake of breath told me I'd done the right thing. "Where?"

"It was *inside* a mint." I explained about Marjatta.

"You've saved my life." He folded the paper around the chip and shoved it into his own pocket. "Literally."

A spear of ice went through me. "Literally? You mean you would have died if I hadn't found this?"

"I might have been tried for treason, so yeah." He smiled. "I owe you, big time."

I snorted. "It's not like you'll be able to repay me. Which reminds me, I could use reimbursement for the train fare."

He pulled a handful of Lunatics out of his pocket. "I'm not sure how much this is, but it's all I've got. And I obviously can't Credi-Send you the credits."

I took the wad of paper and rifled through it. "This is more than enough."

"Good. Look, I really appreciate your help. But if we ever meet in the future, we have to pretend it's the first time. I can't risk blowing my cover."

We stared at each other for a few seconds.

"I guess I'd better go." I put out my fist.

He knocked his knuckles against mine, then grabbed me in a bear hug. "Thanks, Katie Li. I won't forget you." He dropped me as suddenly as he'd grabbed me, his face flushing pink.

"Unless you spray yourself with that ring," I joked weakly.

He turned to the door. "Lock the door after I leave and wait five or ten minutes before you come out. Then go straight home. If anyone follows you, text the word 'pineapple' to this contact." He tapped his Ncuff, and mine buzzed with an incoming contact.

I glanced at the device. An unidentified number appeared on my screen. I saved it under the name Apple, Pine. "What's a pineapple?"

"Ancient Earth fruit." He pushed me gently behind the door so I wouldn't be seen when it opened. "Good luck. And thanks." Then he was gone.

EPISODE 9: HOME OF THE ZERO-GRAVITY WHOOPIE CUSHION

I ANNOUNCED the total to the customer and accepted their payment information. With a smile and my trademark finger wave, I clicked the disconnect button, then took a swig of BublTee. Selling crap to old people was thirsty work. Most younger people ordered directly from their NexUS cuff instead of calling us.

I leaned back in my chair and looked around the room. Twenty agents manned the call center, each of us working from a translucent half-bubble. The caller's face appeared in the center of the bubble. We threw product vids on the curved surface as we worked, running virtual demonstrations to entice the buyers. Sales data scrolled across the bottom half. A small table stuck out of the side—carefully situated out of view of the caller—to give us a place for snacks and beverages. We weren't allowed to eat or drink while on a call, so we had to grab a sip when we could.

My comm pinged, and a red rectangle with the words "incoming call" appeared on the screen. I set my cup aside, checked my teeth, and hit the accept button. "Greetings! You have reached Luna City, LTD. Your call may be monitored for training purposes. My name is Katie. Welcome to the home of the—" A spike of pleased recognition followed by fear rendered me speechless. I stared at my new customer.

Nick Beckett—the long blond hair had been replaced by a dark flattop, but it was definitely him—raised a puzzled eyebrow. "Home of the what?"

Why was he calling me? Or was he? The system automatically assigned customers to the agent who'd been idle for the longest. I glanced around the room again. Betzy was painting her nails and had been for five minutes. Surely, she should have gotten this call?

"Home of the—" my face went hot "—zero-gravity whoopee cushion." I usually gabbled out the intro so automatically that the words didn't register. I hated that our top-selling product reproduced bodily noises for comedy. "Can I add one to your cart?"

His lips twitched. "No, thanks. I'm doing some research for an event I'm planning, and I was hoping you could suggest some products."

He wasn't acknowledging me at all. Well, two could play this game. "If you'll describe your event, sir, perhaps I could offer some."

"My best friend is getting married, and I'm throwing the bachelor party."

I nodded, my stomach sinking. If he wanted to talk to me, he'd chosen the wrong cover story. "We have specialized wedding consultants available to help you with that. May I transfer your call to one of them?"

"I'd rather talk to you," Nick said. "You seem nice, and we've already made a connection."

"I'm not trained in the finer details of wedding planning…"

My supervisor's voice cut in through my earbud. "Take the call, Katie. Seth is out sick, and Narilla is on another call."

"… but if you don't mind it taking a bit longer, I'd be happy to help."

Nick grinned, and a warm wash of pleasure went through me. *Stop that. He's using you for—for who knows what!* I started throwing suggestions from our wedding novelty pages onto the screen, so he could choose the products he wanted.

"I want something classy. Not a drunken brawl with strippers—what's the nicest place in Luna City?"

I paused mid-swipe. "Most people would say the Varian Center." I flicked deeper into our catalog, looking for "classy" bachelor party supplies. But nothing we sold would fit in at the premier event center on the moon. Luna City, LTD, and the Varian Center were two different worlds.

Speaking of which, what was he trying to tell me? He had to be angling at something—I couldn't believe he'd risk calling my company if he was really planning a bachelor party. He'd made it pretty clear our brief collaboration was over. And top secret.

Which was ridiculous. People in Luna City had seen us together. He'd met my friends; he'd spoken to Mother Frane; he'd bought me pastries at a high-end bakery. There was undoubtedly a record of our time together in the Luna City surveillance records. Pretending we'd never met didn't make sense.

Yet, here we were. Maybe he'd forgotten me?

"I don't think Freeze-dried Keg Stands and Moon Police Booty Inspector badges are quite up to the Varian." I flipped through a few more pages.

Nick chuckled. "You might be right. Maybe I should take a look at that place. Do you think they allow visitors?"

"It's a well-known tourist destination. Not in the evenings, of course—they have performances, galas, that sort of thing. But during the day, they do tours. The lunar gravity allows for some spectacular architecture. Are you here in Luna City?"

"I will be next week." He tapped and swiped his Ncuff. "Yeah, I should have time next Tuesday afternoon. How late are the tours? I can't get away from my meetings until almost five."

I opened an external net window and pulled up the Varian Center's page. It wasn't unheard-of for a sales agent to do external research on behalf of a client, but we usually did that for regulars or someone who had placed a large order. A conversation this long without a sale was going to tank my sales stats. I wasn't sure why I was helping him. "It says the last tour is at five-thirty. If you can get there in time?"

"Thank you for your help." He grinned sheepishly. "I could have looked that up myself. What can I do to thank you?"

"I don't suppose you need a case of whoopee cushions?"

"No, but why don't you give me a dozen of those pocket-sized glow-in-the-dark rubber chickens? You can never have too many of those." He tapped one of the items I'd put up on his screen.

I blinked. Why did I suggest rubber chickens for a bachelor party? I'd never get promoted. "One dozen glow-in-the-dark rubber chickens," I confirmed. "And a case of whoopie cushions."

"No, I'll pass on those."

"Are you sure, sir? They're our top-seller." They weren't. In fact, we were pushing them because we had a huge overstock, and no one wanted them. The company was offering a bonus to the agent who sold the most this month.

"Oh, in that case, give me a dozen." He gave the barest eye roll.

I looked deep into his eyes. "They're cheaper by the case, sir. Twenty-four."

Nick sighed. "Give me a case, then."

"You won't regret it, sir." I flicked the case into his checkout bag and glanced at the name field. "Where shall I have these shipped, Citizen Beckett?"

A sly grin crossed his face, and he entered an address. "Can you send that anonymously?"

"Of course, sir." I waited for him to fill in the shipping address, then completed the transaction. "Thank you for choosing Luna City, LTD, Citizen Beckett. May all your gravity be light." It was our standard sign-off, and even when I wasn't trying to impress the caller, it kind of stuck in my throat.

"I appreciate your help, Katie." Nick smiled into my eyes. "I hope to speak with you again… soon. Have a great day." The screen went blank.

I glanced at the clock, then flipped my availability signal to red. Time for a break. I logged out of my desk and took the drop chute to the roof.

Buildings in Luna City were—obviously—inside sealed domes. Most of them didn't have a roof—the buildings extended right up to the overhead shielding. In the older domes, however, there were a few exceptions.

Luna City, LTD, had offices in the oldest dome on Luna, now called "the Hub." This dome had been built to look like a standard town on Lewei—probably to make the residents more comfortable with their new location. As a result, the top floor of each building had half-height walls, like the roof of a terrestrial building. The dome curved overhead to a high arch in the center of the space. We could look across the narrow "streets" to other rooftops.

The roofs originally housed restaurants and bars, but as Luna City grew and they built more modern domes, the rooftop venues had fallen out of favor. My company had rented an office in a building against the Hub's curved outer wall for dirt cheap, and one of the few perks of the job was our rooftop break room. Of course, we shared it with the other businesses in the building, but very few employees seemed to spend time up there.

I stepped out of the drop chute and crossed to my favorite hangout: the spot where the waist-high wall met the curve of the dome. The wall was half a meter wide, so I could sit on the wall, lean against the curve, and watch the pedestrians exit the tunnel from Beijing Dome far below.

That afternoon, the steady stream didn't keep my attention. I stared sightlessly into the distance, wondering about Nick Beckett.

He'd called Luna City, LTD to speak to me. I didn't know how he'd manipulated the system to get his call sent to my desk, and I didn't really care. The fact that he'd done it meant he wanted my help with something. I wasn't sure I was ready to get pulled back into his cloak and dagger world. Three weeks before, when he'd left Luna with his chip, he'd implied we'd never see each other again. And yet, here he was.

He obviously wanted me to meet him at the Varian Center next Tuesday at five-thirty. Did he know I got off work at five, or had he taken a chance? Most businesses on Luna closed at five, so it was a fair guess. He also seemed to assume I'd show up. It would serve him right if I didn't.

Who was I kidding? Of course, I'd be there. The pleasure I'd felt at seeing him again virtually assured I'd be there. Not to mention the instinctive desire to impress him.

I pushed off the wall and stomped across the roof. Just what I needed—a crush on a secret agent.

EPISODE 10: THAT WAS PLAN A

I'D BEEN to the Varian Center before—Marjatta had dragged me to the opening of an art exhibit when we first met. I was an early morning barista at Lunar Coffee then—the one in the Hills. She and some of her high-class friends had dropped in after a night of partying. She'd gone to use the restroom, and her friends had taken off. To be fair, most of them were too drunk to notice they'd left someone behind.

Marjatta had returned to the table, shrugged, and pulled a stool up to the bar to order another mocha latte. The steady stream of commuter customers had dropped off, and the tourist trade was still at least two hours away, so we chatted while I cleaned the equipment and made the occasional Lunar Macchiato.

Marjatta was from one of the oldest and wealthiest families in Luna City. She'd finished college on Lewei a few months earlier, then returned to her family—without the high ranking Leweian husband they'd sent her to find. Her degree in comparative ancient media—and her complete lack of interest in earning a living—meant she had lots of time on her hands.

About two weeks after we met, she took me to the art opening. She loaned me a dress—which was a good thing because the fanciest clothing I owned would have made me look like one of the human wait-staff's destitute cousins. We'd had a great time joking about the paintings and quietly mocking the other guests. I'd even met a few of her wealthy friends, but they were drunk again, and boorish.

Now, I stared up at the soaring architecture. The Varian Center occupied a dome of its own. The transparent top—like in the Hills—provided a spectacular view of space, with Lewei a blue-green sphere in the west. The building's huge, onion-shaped dome towered above the wide plaza in front, the spire nearly touching the thick stone ceiling.

The Varian Center was built by the Varian family who literally owned Luna before the first settlements went up. They'd continued to build their fortune renting property—and selling oxygen—to the new inhabitants. After the cultural revolution, the Leweian government had wrested control of the moon from the grip of the oligarchy, and the Varians had ended their days in the Xinjianestan educational camp. The building was officially renamed *Honor and Glory to the People of Lewei Hall*, but everyone—including the government—still called it the Varian Center. We weren't quite as hard-core as the people of Lewei.

I walked across the wide plaza and stopped by a small kiosk to buy a ticket for the tour. I checked my account balance and made a mental note to ask Nick for reimbursement. Touring this place cost a fortune. I'd taken the tour before, of course—the Luna City schools had mandatory field trips to places of cultural significance. But that was funded by the school. The tourist ticket cost more than my rent.

Not really, but it felt like it.

As we filed across the plaza, I scanned the tour group, but Nick was not with us. I chewed on my lip as the tour guide gave the same spiel I'd heard in grades two, seven, and twelve, about the corruption of the Varian family and the benevolence of the Leweian government. We obediently admired the fine lunar stone under our feet—the same lunar stone that was used to build nearly everything in Luna City, including the thick domes shielding us from the thin atmosphere outside. Then we marched across that fine lunar stone to enter the building.

The main doors opened on a wide hall. The floor was paved with—unsurprisingly—more fine lunar stone. Soaring arches supported galleries carved and painted with scenes of the cultural revolution. No one mentioned what scenes had originally graced these walls—I figured it was Varian family portraits or maybe piles of gold to denote their wealth.

The guide opened the double doors leading through a narrow corridor—narrow for a building this size but wide enough for three people to walk abreast. At the far end of this short tunnel, she paused dramatically, then flung open the interior doors. The crowd oohed and ahhed as they flooded inside.

A hand grabbed my arm and yanked me into a dark alcove and through a narrow door marked "staff." I bit back a yelp and stumbled into the black room. The dim light from the hallway outside barely touched the stygian shadows. The hand let go, and the door clicked shut behind me, leaving me alone in the pitch-dark.

"Hello?" My heartbeat thudded in my ears, increasing in tempo and volume as I waited for an answer. I put my hands out, feeling for a wall, a pillar, anything. I hit something solid and warm.

Someone stepped close, the heat radiating from his body giving me a sense of size. Fingers pressed against my lips, and warm breath tickled my ear. "This way." The hand left my mouth, sliding down my shoulder and arm to grasp my wrist. A gentle tug started me moving.

I blundered through the darkness, keeping my free hand out to hopefully stop me from slamming into anything. Another door opened ahead, then closed behind us. Finally, a NexUs cuff glowed. The dim light blinded me for a second. I blinked a few times, then saw Nick.

"Thanks for coming," he said in a soft whisper. The faint rasp in his deep drawl sent shivers up my spine. "No one followed you, did they?"

"Why would anyone follow me?" My voice came out high and squeaky. I coughed and tried to shift to a lower register—one humans could actually hear. "I came alone."

A grin flickered across his face and disappeared. "Perfect. I need your help."

I took a second to look around. We stood in a small office—standard desk with a screen much like my bubble at LCL, cabinets with drawers along one wall, a board covered with handwritten notes and tacked-up papers. I tried to hit on something clever to say, but ended up with, "With what?"

He released my wrist and tapped his Ncuff.

My arm felt cold and alone. *Stop that, you besotted idiot.*

My Ncuff vibrated, and an event invitation appeared, notifying me of a charity auction to be held here at the Varian on Friday. "What is this?"

"It's an event I have to attend. I need to meet a contact, and I need a cover. You're going to be my date."

"I thought we were supposed to pretend we didn't know each other."

"That was plan A." Nick smiled, and that now familiar warm wave ran through me. "But I've come to realize having you here is a perfect cover. I can come to visit without anyone suspecting—I'm just here to see my girl." His arm slid around me and pulled me close.

I put a hand against his chest, holding him off. "You want me to pretend to be your girlfriend so you can visit Luna City without anyone suspecting you're a spy."

"Operative, not spy. And I'm not sure I'm ready to commit to an exclusive relationship." He winked. "But yeah. Close enough."

I tried to step back, but his arm held me like a steel band. When I pushed against his chest, he released me immediately. I stumbled backward, catching my balance against the desk. "What's in it for me?"

"Besides my sparkling personality?"

I raised my nose in the air and tried to channel Marjatta's mother. "Yeah, besides that. I don't normally have to work so hard for male companionship."

His lips twitched. "I'm playing the role of a highly-placed Leweian tourist. I can shower you with Reanta's beignets and black-tie events."

"Why didn't you say so?" I made my eyes as wide as possible and batted my eyelashes. "Which brings up another problem. I don't have the appropriate clothing for an event at the Varian Center. I could borrow something from Marjatta…"

He held up a hand. "Don't tell her about this."

"She's going to see us at the venue." I waved at the invitation still showing on my Ncuff. "This is the kind of thing her family attends all the time."

"What's her surname?"

"Lipinski."

His eyes flickered with surprise, and I could see the calculations ticking away inside his brain. "That could be…fortuitous. Will you introduce me?"

"You met her at my party, but she probably doesn't remember you." That was a lie. Despite the enormous amount of alcohol she'd consumed, Nick was the one thing she had remembered.

"That didn't answer my question." His eyes bored into mine.

"Why do you want to meet her?"

"She's from one of the first families of Luna City. She'll have contacts I could never make on my own."

"Maybe you should fake-date her instead." I crossed my arms as a ridiculous wave of depression poured through me.

The calculating look returned to Nick's face. "Maybe I should. But she can't know who I am or what I do."

"No. That's where I draw the line." I poked my finger into Nick's rock-solid chest. He didn't even flinch. "You can fake-date me, but if you make a move on Marjatta, I *will* blow your cover. I'm not letting you use her that way. She gets enough jerks hitting on her who only want her status and connections. I'm not letting you do that."

His warm hand closed around mine, pulling my finger away from his solar plexus. "Deal. I won't hit on Marjatta, and you don't tell her about me."

I drew my hand away. "Not so fast. I still have some demands."

EPISODE 11: YOU COULD HAVE ASKED FOR TWICE AS MUCH

NICK SMILED AT ME. "So, we're agreed. I pay for your entrance ticket to the Varian—"

"And any other expenses I incur in the future. If I'm going to have to visit cultural sites to meet you, the demands will exceed my income very quickly."

"Any other expenses within reason—I'm not buying you a whole new wardrobe."

I lifted my chin. "No caveats. I'll try to borrow clothes from Marjatta, but there might be times that isn't possible. You're going to have to trust me to be reasonable. This relationship is built on trust, right?"

Nick laughed. "You're too good at negotiation. How about this—I will give you an allowance during any month we work together. Paid in Lunites, so it can't be traced." He pulled out a wad of high-value notes and handed them to me. "Is that enough?"

I gulped. That was more than I made in a week. "Deal."

He bumped his fist against mine. "Just so you know, you could have asked for twice that much."

"Just so you know, I would have done it for half."

———

Friday was the longest workday of my life. It started out slowly, with very few calls coming through to my bubble. Unlike Betzy, I couldn't stand the smell of nail polish, and we weren't allowed to skim the web, so I spent the empty moments reorganizing my virtual files. I archived my sales from last year, deleted my scratch pad files, and purged my partially complete orders—those customers were never coming back, and if they did, our inventory had changed.

After lunch, the calls picked up, and before I knew it, my break reminder pinged. As I locked my system for a short respite on the roof, a message came in from Prentice, my supervisor. "See me asap." I sighed and grabbed my iced coffee.

His door was open, so I knocked against the doorjamb. "You wanted to see me?"

"Katie, good." Prentice shuffled through a pile of paper—who uses that stuff anymore?—as he motioned me in. He was an older man with thinning gray hair and dark circles around his eyes, as if he never got enough sleep. He was also hopelessly out of touch with technology. "I was looking at your stats." He brandished a page.

He printed my stats? This was exactly what I was talking about.

I slowly lowered myself onto the edge of a chair. I wasn't due for an evaluation until next month, and my sales numbers were trending up this week. I watched my stats obsessively, since outperforming my peers was the only avenue to promotion. I didn't want to answer calls for the rest of my life. "Is this a review session?"

He waved the paper again and jammed a bite of sandwich into his mouth. "No." Crumbs flew across the desk as he spoke around the food, and he brushed them away. "I wanted to talk to you about Tuesday's call." He set the page in front of me and tapped a line.

It was my call with Nick. Crap. I knew that was going to haunt me. "He wasn't ready to order—"

He cut me off. "Excellent job on the cross-sale. You sold more whoopie cushions than anyone else this week, on that sale alone."

I went cold in mild panic. "He didn't cancel the order, did he?"

"What? Why would he do that? You did good. Product shipped from our warehouse on Lewei yesterday. Well done. The warehouse called me to double check the delivery address, but it matched the call transcript, so I told them to send it."

I bit my lip. Nick had had the whoopie cushions shipped to the home of the Premier of Lewei. I was sure the address would be flagged by the system, and I guess in a way it had been. But LCL didn't care where the stuff went, as long as the charges went through. And the Premier had a kid, so it would be fine, right?

The last hours of the day flew by. I was having second, third, and fourth thoughts about going to the Varian Center with Nick. Eating beignets with him was one thing, but pretending to be his girlfriend as a cover for who knew what mayhem was making my stomach hurt.

I swallowed the last of my iced coffee, feeling jittery and nauseated. I probably should have skipped the fourth one, but free drinks were one of the few perks of this job, and when I was hired, I had promised myself I'd take full advantage of that.

Marjatta had given me free reign in her closet, with the caveat that I get dressed at her place. After work, I slung my tote bag over my shoulder and boarded the train to Paris Dome.

Most of the high-ranking families lived in Paris, Beijing, and Hua Hin. These domes offered larger apartments, more modern recreational facilities, and direct trains to the shuttle port. Plus, unlike the rest of the city, the tunnels between them were regularly cleared of the homeless population.

The train dropped me in a blindingly white station with sparkling clean floors and a human attendant. I wasn't sure what his function was, except maybe to be a deterrent to those who didn't belong. He looked me over in slow contempt, but when I didn't turn and run, he made no attempt to stop me.

I hiked my bag a little more securely on my shoulder, raised my nose into the air, and stalked past him to the slide ramp.

At the top, I entered the wide corridors of Paris Dome and turned right. High-end shops flanked both sides of the main corridor, their expensive goods on display behind tall windows. The ceiling soared high above me, held up by graceful arches. Ahead, the central concourse, like in Beijing, stood in a multi-level atrium.

I'd been here enough times that I no longer gaped like a tourist when I arrived, but only through sheer force of will. Even after two years of friendship with Marjatta, I couldn't believe she lived in all this glitz.

I walked across the wide concourse. The drop chute took me to the sixth floor. The Lipinskis' compartment was the first on the right—a prime location with easy access to the center. I waved my hand at the access panel, and moments later, the door swung open.

A short, thin man with thick, white hair bowed and stepped aside for me to enter. "Good evening, Citizen Li. It is very nice to see you again. Lady Marjatta is expecting you."

Lady Marjatta Lipinski. That was her official title. She wasn't nobility or royalty—we didn't have that in the Lewei system. But officials who rank high in the political sphere, like Marjata's parents, were granted titles, as were their children. Marjatta's father was Grand Baron Lipinksi, and her mother was a Grand Baroness, although she prefered to use her military rank.

"Thanks, Kerdin. Is she in her room?" I stepped onto the polished stone floor of the large entry and stepped to one side. There, I slid my shoes off and slipped my feet into the waiting slippers.

Kerdin nodded and pushed open the double doors that led to the private area of the apartment. "Have a pleasant evening, Citizen."

The public parts of the apartment contained the formal dining room, a massive gathering space, smaller parlor, theater, gym, and access to the government areas of the dome which included secure offices and recreational facilities as well as the private train station with a direct connection to the shuttle port.

But the family had a separate section for everyday use. I paced along the plush carpet, swiftly passing the doors to the family parlor and dining room, then the grand baron's office and the admiral's study. Marjatta had given me a full tour of the apartment one day when her parents were planet-side. The place was huge. Past the two offices were her parents' separate bedrooms, each with a private bath, an additional sitting room, and a wet bar. Beyond those were Marjatta's large sitting room and even larger bedroom, also with a full bath.

I knocked on Marjatta's door and pushed it open without waiting for her reply. Her sitting room used to be the nursery when she was a child. As she aged, it had been redecorated several times. Now, the walls were a warm cream color, with coppery brown carpet on the floor. Comfortable furniture grouped around a huge viewing screen on one side, while a desk, chairs, and a full wall of shelves took up the other. The shelves held decorative knickknacks and a few old-fashioned paper books. Not that Marjatta ever read any of them —they were antiques, valued for their age and their previous owners. She'd once showed me a book that had been owned by the fourth premier before she was disgraced and executed.

As I entered, Marjatta jumped up, throwing her e-reader on the couch. In public, Marjatta played the role of bored socialite to perfection, but in private, she preferred reading to partying. "You're finally here! Let's get started." She wore a pink bath robe and curlers in her hair.

She hustled me into the bedroom and flicked her Ncuff. With a swift look at the clock, she pointed me toward the bathroom. "Shower. There's a robe in there for you. Don't get your hair wet—Francois says it's easier to style if it isn't clean."

I dropped my bag on the floor and followed instructions. A few minutes later, I sat in front of a huge mirror, wrapped in a blue robe, combing out my still-dry hair. Marjatta handed me a glass. I sniffed. "Smells alcoholic."

"It is." She clinked her glass against mine. "Just a little, to help you relax. You're as jittery as a mung-bird."

I sipped the beverage, the gingery bubbles tingling against my tongue. I swallowed, warmth flowing into my stomach. "Nice. I think I had too much coffee today."

"It's a big night—you don't usually date the kind of guys who go to the Varian." She took the comb from my hand and went to work on my hair. "Is this your planet guy?"

"Yeah, the guy I met at Milo's. He's coming back this week and wanted a companion at the deal so he wouldn't be attacked by every unattached woman in the room. Not that he said that," I added when she gave me a strange look. "He wouldn't say that about himself, but that's what would happen. He is Hawaiian Thor, after all."

"As long as he doesn't wear the shirt." She tapped the comb against her cheek. "What does 'Hawaiian' mean anyway? Is it a brand of shirt?"

I shrugged. "Ya got me. It's what they call that big flower print. Maybe Thor knows."

"Do not ask Planet Guy—I can guarantee you he doesn't know and doesn't care. He wore the shirt because he looks hot in it, not because it's named after Rylie Hawa. Or whatever."

"Who is Rylie Hawa?"

She picked up her drink and took a sip. "No idea. I just made it up. What's his name?"

"Rylie?" She gave me a blank look. "Whose name?"

"Your planet guy's, of course."

My mind went blank. What name was Nick using for this visit? John Smith? Nick Beckett? Something totally different? He could be going by Rylie Hawa, for all I knew.

I was *so* not made for subterfuge.

EPISODE 12: SOAP. I NEED SOAP

BECKETT.

He used Nick Beckett for the LCL purchase, so that must be the name he was using here. "His name is Nick."

A quiet ping alerted us to a new arrival. The name Francois Zendas appeared on the screen by the door. Marjatta flicked her NexUs-Cuff, and the door opened. A tall man with flowing red hair swept into the suite, followed by a drab woman pulling a large, wheeled case.

"Lady Marjatta! I am honored to be in your presence once again." The man made a complicated bow toward my friend, then a tiny nod at me. "Citizen Li."

"Citizen Zendas." I hadn't mastered the technique of putting someone in their place simply by uttering their name, but I attempted to mimic Zendas's tone. He ignored me.

"Francois, I want you to start with Katie's hair." Marjatta waved the comb at me. "When you're done with hers, you can put mine up."

"But Lady Marjatta, you know your sensitive tresses require time and finesse—"

She cut him off. "Do hers first."

With an elegant flounce, Francois took the comb and turned away. "Dewi, attend to Lady Marjatta."

While Francois yanked the comb through my hair and pinned it up, Dewi worked on Marjatta's makeup. When he'd finished my updo, Francois supervised Dewi, ordering her to try different things, although it was all said in tones that sounded like mere suggestions.

Passive-aggressive much, Zendas?

Dewi's face tightened, then visibly relaxed into a serene expression. When she finished Marjatta's eyelashes, she backed away, bowing.

Francois gave Marjatta a critical once-over. "It's a bit pale. But I guess that's the trend now. You've done well enough, Dewi."

"I think it looks amazing, Dewi." Marjatta turned her face back and forth, watching in the wrap-around mirrors. "The contouring is remarkable. Thank you."

Francois bustled forward. "I'll tone that down. Nothing should be remarkable—a lady's makeup should be so perfect that it's unnoticeable. You'll have to complete the eye design training again, Dewi." With that, he turned Marjatta's chair, so he stood between us and her.

I caught Dewi's eyes in the mirror. "I thought it looked lovely," I whispered.

"Thank you, Citizen," she breathed. "Please close your eyes and relax."

I leaned back in the chair and let her work.

I tried to relax, but the massive amount of caffeine coursing through my veins made that impossible. As Dewi painted my face, I clicked my string of stone worry beads between my fingers, while my mind raced.

Nick hadn't given me much information about tonight. From what little he had said, my role was to help him present a normal appearance. A single man from Lewei was sure to be noticed and commented on while a couple would blend in with all the others.

But why was he attending? Was he meeting with another agent or an informer? Was he passing secret messages? Would he expect me to hang on his arm and laugh at his jokes, or would he abandon me to find his contact? And agents were usually armed, weren't they? I wracked my brains, pulling every spy vid I'd ever seen out of memory. Guns were illegal in Luna City, but should I have a set of brass knuckles or a sword?

I stifled a snort of near-hysterical laughter. A sword. What was I thinking? A sword-shaped letter opener was more my style. I thought we sold those at LCL. I made a mental note to check the catalog.

Dewi finished the eyeliner, so I sat forward to grab my drink. I downed the last of it and looked in the mirror.

"Wow." My thick brown hair had been rolled into a smooth chignon on the back of my head. A few wisps curled around my face—a face that was almost unrecognizable. Dewi had applied contouring that transformed my round cheeks. I had cheekbones! And the shading around my eyes made them sparkle.

"Let me do the lashes." Dewi pushed me back in the chair. "Look up, please. Now down. Wait. Now, blink. Perfect." She handed me my glass which had magically refilled.

I stared at my reflection. "You're a genius, Dewi."

The girl beamed with pleasure. "The citizen has excellent bone structure."

I smirked. "Yeah, if you like round. I can't believe…you're an artist."

Francois turned at that. He looked in the mirror, then did a double-take. As he stalked toward us, Dewi spun my chair to face him. "Not terrible." Then he stepped to the side and flourished his arms dramatically. "Behold true artistry."

Marjatta rose from her chair. Her hair was…indescribable. There were loops and curls and some zig-zag sections sticking out at gravity-defying angles. Expensive-looking jewelry was woven into the mass of blond and brown. A huge tear-shaped ruby hung on her forehead, just above her brows. Francois had added some faceted stones to the corners of her eyes and glitter to her lips. The effect was mesmerizing but not in a good way.

Dewi and I squealed. Mine might have started as a scream of horror, but I attempted to change my grimace to a sickly smile. "That is incredible. You look amazing. Francois, you are a…"

"Genius? Yes, I am."

Marjatta stared in the mirror, appalled.

I took a gulp and came to her rescue. "I thought a lady's makeup was supposed to be unnoticeable?"

Francois waved this away. "That is for ordinary citizens. A woman of Lady Marjatta's status should be bold, dramatic, a trendsetter!"

Dewi, Marjatta, and I exchanged a look. He'd clearly said Dewi overdid Marjatta's makeup earlier.

Francois dropped a brush on the dressing table, splashing virulent pink powder across the polished surface. "I must be off. I have an appointment with Baroness Hightower. Kiss, kiss." This last bit was said in Marjatta's direction, and Francois disappeared out the door.

Marjatta lunged for the bathroom. "Soap. I need soap."

"Let me help you." Dewi guided Marjatta back to the chair in front of her dressing table. "I can…hang on." She pulled a small bag out of her larger one and went to work. Dewi removed half of the jewelry from my friend's hair and smoothed out the most angular bits. She wiped the glitter and bright colors off Marjatta's face, allowing her natural beauty to shine through. "It's still a little out there but not as bad."

I walked around Marjatta, observing from all angles. "It's much better— and not changed enough to get you in trouble. You're the genius. Why do you work for him?"

"He's the 'in' hair designer," Marjatta answered for Dewi. "Francois's repu- tation gets her into the highest status houses. As he gets more flamboyant, she'll pick up clients among the more conservative and eventually take his place."

"I don't want to take Francois's business!" Dewi held both hands up in protest. "We're a team—he does hair, I do makeup."

Marjatta smirked at me. "Trust me, I've seen it before. And in a few years, you'll have to amp up the crazy to stay on the radars of the most powerful—and your assistant will clean up after you. Then she'll eclipse you. It's the natural order. If you're smart, you'll save your credits, and by then, you'll be ready to retire and won't care."

"Unlike Francois," Dewi muttered, then clapped her hands over her mouth. "I didn't say that."

Marjatta smiled kindly. "Say what? Thanks for the amazing job. I've sent your payment already."

Dewi quickly packed away all the equipment she and Francois had used, then hesitated near the door. "Do you wish assistance getting dressed?"

Marjatta waved her away. "We've got this. You've got other clients, I'm sure."

"I need to get to Baroness Hightower's before Francois finishes her hair. Thank you, Lady Marjatta, Citizen Li." The door snicked shut behind her.

"How is Francois doing Baroness Hightower's hair if he left all his stuff here?"

Marjatta unzipped the garment bag holding her new gown. "He has his kit shipped to clients' homes in advance. The stuff Dewi just carted away has been here since early this morning. I'm sure he has multiple sets."

"And poor Dewi has to clean up after him."

Marjatta shrugged. "Start at the bottom, work your way up. That's what a good citizen does."

"Like you?" I snickered.

She paused, considering. "Some of us get to take the fast track. It's nice to have parents who put in the work for you."

"Not really equal treatment, though." The Lewei government always claimed to treat all citizens equally, but as my mother used to say, some were more equal than others.

"Are we going to debate politics, or are we going to a party?" Marjatta slid the cover away from a waterfall of diamonds.

"That is—my brain can't even wrap around what's happening here." I reached out a finger to touch the glittering cascade but pulled it back. "How is that a dress?"

Marjatta pulled the glittering lower edge away from the wall and handed it to me. "Hold the hem."

I took the bottom of the dress and stepped back. Marjatta ducked under my arm and squirmed up into the dress. She slid the hanger out of the neckline as she shimmied in, and suddenly, she was clothed in a transparent sheath of diamonds. She tossed the hanger aside and turned. "What do you think?"

My brain refused to click into gear. The dress appeared to be transparent, but I couldn't see her body through the fabric. Parts of it matched her skin tone exactly. The fall of diamonds streamed over her breasts and across her hips, hiding all the private bits from view. As she turned, the fan of sparkles over her butt glinted in the lights. The dress was beautiful but disturbing—making me feel like an unwitting voyeur. The sparkles imitated water, as if she just stepped out of the shower. She spun, and the skirt flared, her legs visible between flashes of diamond.

I gaped, mesmerized.

She smiled, like a satisfied feline. "Perfect." She flopped down on the small couch and gestured to another bag. "Put yours on."

I unzipped the second bag and pulled out a deep red dress. I'd coveted this gown for months, so when Marjatta offered me free reign of her closet, I'd jumped on the opportunity. I tried it on a couple of days before, and despite our very different figures, it looked fantastic on both of us.

Following her lead, I ducked under the hem and squirmed into the gown. The fitted bodice drooped loose on my shoulders. "Can you fasten the back?"

She jumped up and pressed the closure in one smooth movement. I turned to look in the mirror. The top clung to my figure, emphasizing my narrow waist. The deep neckline gave me a sexier look than my flat chest usually offered. The full skirt swirled around my ankles. I tapped my Ncuff, and my shoes darkened to match the color.

Marjatta clapped and cooed. "Perfect! When did you say you'd meet him?"

I glanced at my Ncuff. "Crap! Twenty minutes ago!"

EPISODE 13: WALKING THE GAUNTLET

"TWENTY MINUTES LATE IS PERFECT." Marjatta pulled open the door and swept out of the bedroom. "Always make them wait."

I hurried after her, out of the private section of the home and across the wide lobby to the public area. She waved her diamond-inlaid, twenty-four-carat gold Ncuff at the access panel, and strolled into the gathering space.

As we entered, Kerdin cleared his throat ostentatiously, and the rumble of conversation stopped dead. "Lady Marjatta Lipinski." People turned to look, and a murmur went around the room.

The place was packed with men and women in evening dress. Marjatta sailed through the crowd, pausing only long enough to air kiss her mother and exchange a few words here and there. I followed in her wake, noticing the envious glares from the men and women she ignored. Every one of them would undoubtedly look me up later to see who gained the favor of Lady Marjatta this week.

That was one of the reasons I didn't usually attend events with her. The first time we went to a play, one of her "friends" decided I was a threat to their relationship. She tracked me down later and made vague but believable threats against my employment and even my liberty. Could she really frame me for extortion? It wasn't a chance I wanted to take.

But after I'd agreed to go with Nick, I needed Marjatta's help with the dress. I could have taken the gown home and skipped this part of the ordeal, but if my friend was going to kit me out, the least I could do was keep her company as she walked the gauntlet.

People crowded around her, pushing into me. Someone stepped on the hem of my dress. Someone else bumped into me, and I stumbled. A hand slapped against my arm, hard, and gripped, stopping my fall.

Marjatta turned and held out a hand to me. "Come on, Katie." She pulled me beside her, and we pushed through the throng.

We reached the far end of the compartment and paused before a pair of wide doors. They swished open in response to Marjatta's Ncuff, and we stepped into a mini-pod. She took the plush, double seat on one side, and I sat on the other, leaving plenty of room for my wide skirt. As the doors closed, I glanced back at the crowd in the gathering room. "Aren't they coming?"

Marjatta shrugged. "They'll be along later."

"But it starts in ten minutes. Don't they want to mingle—or be seen on the red carpet—before?"

She snorted. "They're probably wondering why we went so early. Nothing important will happen before my parents get there. I'm amazed Planet Guy insisted on meeting so early."

"He's from off-world. He doesn't know how these things work. I've heard people on Lewei are sticklers for punctuality."

"Really?"

"No. I don't know why he wanted me there so early—except maybe he figured I'd be late, and he didn't want to miss the beginning." He probably wanted me there early to cover for some clandestine discussion with a contact. Maybe I've blown the whole operation by being late.

In which case, he should have clued me in beforehand. Totally his fault.

"It's an art exhibit. Even if the artist is there, she isn't going to speak at the exact moment the building opens. And this is Jiangia—not exactly the most reliable guest of honor. She came to a dinner my dad held—she was three hours late. Half the attendees were getting ready to leave when she arrived."

That likely wasn't true—no one would leave Baron Lipinski's house before the guest of honor showed up.

The pod slid to a halt, and the doors opened. Lights flashed as Marjatta stepped out. She raised an elegant hand to acknowledge the ranks of paparazzi, then turned to pose in front of the pod with a brilliant smile. After a brief pause for pictures, she beckoned to me, and we strode up a red runner to the front door. There, she turned again. I stepped aside to allow her to pose in front of the billboard emblazoned with "Jiangia" and the Varian Center logo, then followed her inside.

Well-dressed people crowded the lobby. These were the upper-middle-class attempting to network with the top ranks. They'd wait here until the barons and admirals arrived, then swarm them with offers of drinks and favors. Eventually, the invited guests would filter inside, and the rest would wait outside until the show ended.

A half-dozen conservatively dressed men and women surrounded Marjatta.

I was hastily evaluated, instantly relegated to "hanger-on," and pushed aside. The crowd eddied and swirled away with Marjatta at its center, leaving me like trash washed up on the beach.

"Hi." Hawaiian Thor appeared at my shoulder, holding two glasses of a pale bubbling beverage. "Drink?"

I took the glass with a nod and looked him over. He wore a dark suit with a narrow collar over a white shirt. A small oval of shiny black stone—obsidian or something similar—glinted at the base of his throat between the white points. His dark flattop stood at attention, perfectly level. He looked amazing.

"Nice dress." His eyes flickered over my body and back to my face. "You clean up good."

"Thanks, so do you." I hunched my shoulders and glanced at Marjatta. "I had help."

He sipped his drink and wrinkled his nose. "What is this?"

"Moonshine. Luna City specialty."

"It's...bland."

"But it packs a punch—at least for us locals."

"That's right, someone told me Lunites are lightweights." His eyes twinkled.

"Was that me?" I don't remember saying it, but it sounded like me.

He nodded. "Let's stroll around the room, shall we?" He poked his elbow at me.

I glanced at his arm in confusion, then poked mine toward him so our elbows bumped.

He laughed. "You're supposed to hold my arm." He took my hand and looped it through the crook of his arm.

"Why?" I stuck out my foot so he could see my dark red flats. "I'm not wearing heels, and I'm not an invalid."

He patted my fingers. "It's a Leweian thing, I guess. I'm escorting you to the show."

I yanked my hand away. "I am not an escort. And I'm certainly not going to pay for one!"

"Relax." His warm hand closed around my fingers and pulled them through his arm again. "I meant escort as in 'taking you someplace.' Not hiring you for a night of passion. Although I wouldn't be averse to—"

I tried to pull away again, but his hand held mine tightly.

"I'm kidding. Lighten up. We've got a mission, and you're drawing too much attention."

"Yeah, about this mission—how about you fill me in? What's going to happen?"

"You're going to introduce me to your friend." He steered me across the room toward the scrum surrounding Marjatta.

"I thought you had some other mission—you didn't come here to meet Marjatta. You didn't even know I knew her until I told you who she was." I hung back, slowing his purposeful stride.

"You're right, I didn't. After we speak to Marjatta, we'll go into the exhibit hall and look at the paintings. At some point, my contact will approach me. You'll excuse yourself to use the powder room, and I'll do what I need to do. When you come back, we'll look at the art some more. Then I'll see you home."

"That's all you want me to do? Go to the restroom?" I stared at him for a moment, then recalled my surroundings and looked at the ceiling as if fascinated by the architecture.

He pulled on my arm, and I tripped into him. "Oops." I giggled. "Good thing I didn't spill the booze." I finished my drink and looked for someplace to put the empty glass.

"You are an *extreme* lightweight." He took the glass and handed it to one of the human waitstaff. When she offered a replacement, he refused. "Take me to meet your friend."

I nodded. I had a mission—time to carry it out. I dropped his elbow and grabbed his hand, yanking him forward. "Excuse me." I tapped the closest shoulder. As the guy turned, I pushed between him and the woman next to him. "Excuse me. Coming through. Pardon."

Nick dragged at my arm. "Katie, we don't need to make a scene."

I glared at him over my shoulder. "You want to meet my friend. I want you to meet my friend. She wants to meet you. Come on." I snapped around and pushed between two more people. "Excuse me."

"Katie." A yank on my hand sent me sprawling into Nick's arms. He caught me and swung me out of the crowd, setting me on my feet behind a wide pillar.

"Wow, you are strong." I reached up and squeezed his bicep. "Like steel."

"You can't possibly be this drunk from one watered-down glass of booze." He leaned down to peer into my eyes. "Are you okay?"

"I feel fabulous." I did—kind of floaty and impervious. The nervousness from earlier had disappeared. I didn't know if it was the drink or if being around Nick simply intoxicated me. I spun around. "Don't I look fabulous?" Nick caught my arm, and I winced. "Ow."

He turned me sharply and looked at my upper arm. "There's blood here. Did you hurt yourself?"

I twisted my neck, trying to look at the back of my upper arm. "That's where someone slapped me. At Marjatta's house." I tilted in the direction of my twist, the floor coming toward my face at an alarming rate. Or it would have been alarming if I hadn't felt so warm and cozy.

Nick caught me before I hit the floor. "Someone drugged you."

EPISODE 14: NO ONE DRUGGED ME BEFORE I MET YOU

NICK FROWNED AT MY ARM. "This looks like a stinger."

"Like from a bug?"

"It's a drug administered via a tiny, multi-prong device. It leaves a small circular mark with multiple punctures. Very distinctive. Someone drugged you."

"Not again." I stumbled, trying to adjust myself to the waves rocking the floor beneath my feet.

"Again? What do you mean?" His voice was sharp.

"First you, now someone else. I don't think I like working with you if this is what happens." A wave of exhaustion washed over me. I blinked slowly, trying to keep my eyes open. "Or at least I need to take a nap first."

"This couldn't have anything to do with me." He slid an arm around my waist and directed me toward the inner doors. "We'll find someplace for you to rest."

"Of course it has to do with you." I stepped carefully into the undulating hall. "No one drugged me before I met you."

"Sh. Keep your voice down. We can't draw attention." He looked around, then opened one of the thick doors and ushered me inside.

The exhibit hall was empty. Huge canvasses covered the walls, bright with random splashes of paint. Eyes peeked from behind thick green splotches here, more eyes blinked between purple and yellow stripes there. The floor vibrated, and the walls hummed. "This is the weirdest art I've ever seen."

"Jiangia is experimental post-neo-interpretive, according to the advertisement." He steered me across the room to a short hallway. A quick press against a blank section of wall and a door slid aside. We stepped in. "This is the ladies' room. Why don't you lie down on that couch for a few minutes? I'll have someone check on you in a bit."

He pulled his arm away, and I swayed, blinking owlishly at the sofa. "Are you trying to ditch me?"

"Not at all. But this is the ladies' room. I can't stay in here."

I dropped onto the seat, then reached up to grab his hand. "Stay." I yanked hard. He didn't budge.

"I can't."

"Right. The mission." I put a finger to my lips and looked around the room to make sure no one was listening.

He groaned. "You are drunk. I'm going to leave you here to sleep it off. Do not talk to anyone."

Tears burned in my eyes. "You're dumping me because I'm drunk!" I bit back a howl of despair.

"Katie, hush." He dropped beside me on the sofa and put his arm around me again. "I'm not dumping you. Just close your eyes for a few minutes, then we'll go to the exhibit."

I leaned my head against his shoulder and let my eyes drift shut. "I'm not drunk. I only had one moonshine. Don't leave me. I need you." His arm, warm and solid, squeezed gently. I snuggled in close, letting the couch rock beneath me, lulling me to sleep.

————

My eyes popped open, and I sat up. I was alone in a small room, lying on a tufted green couch. A damp spot marked where I'd drooled on the upholstery. I groaned and stood, my head spinning, then settling.

After a second, the events of the evening came into sharp focus: Marjatta, Nick, the unsteady floor. I groaned in embarrassment.

The floor held steady as I crossed the room. I stepped in front of a full-length mirror, turning to look at the back of my arm. The mark Nick had pointed out had faded to a pale pink circle against my brown skin. I pushed against the mark, wincing at the soreness. Who had drugged me? No one at Marjatta's could have known I was helping Nick, so why?

Probably one of her dumb groupies mad that I was her BFF. I knew attending this deal with her was a risk, but I had no idea they'd stoop to drugging me. And what was the point? Just to embarrass me? Luckily, Nick had been there to limit the damage.

Nick! Where was he? Did he need my help? I took a quick look in the mirror to make sure my nap hadn't damaged my dress, hair, or makeup, then hurried out the door.

The venue was full. Hundreds of people in glittering dresses and perfectly tailored suits swirled around me. I spotted a couple of the guests from Marjatta's house and ducked behind a pillar. I didn't need another dose of stinger.

I wandered around the edge of the event, carefully avoiding the guests who filled the center of the room. None of them appeared to be looking at the paintings displayed along the walls. After a quick look, I could see why. The huge canvas next to me depicted a dark alleyway with an enormous, dripping splotch of red across it. It looked like blood, and it actually dripped into a narrow trough on the floor.

Ew.

I looked toward the center of the room, moving from pillar to pillar around the outside of the enormous gallery. A sea of bodies filled the space. Taking a quick look to make sure no one was watching, I climbed onto a padded bench beneath a—non-dripping—painting. Due to his height and breadth, Nick's dark flattop should have been visible above most of the guests, but there was no sign of him. I stepped down and moved to another bench at the far end of the room. Still no joy.

"Are you looking for someone?" a smooth voice asked. I turned to see a slender man with receding ginger hair and a kind of scrunched nose. His lightly lined face looked familiar, but I couldn't place him.

"My friend is here somewhere." I tried to laugh lightheartedly, but it came out as a nervous giggle. "We got separated by the crowd."

The man held out his elbow. "Perhaps if you tell me who your friend is, I can return you to him."

My brain spun. I wasn't supposed to tell people about Nick. "Her." My voice was as nervous sounding as the giggle. "My friend is Lady Marjatta Lipinski."

The man blinked. "You travel in lofty circles. I'm Endral Warenton. We met in the park a few weeks ago."

"In the park?" I frowned, trying to remember. He must mean the Hills—so obviously he wasn't a local. No one called it the park. But the last time I'd been in the Hills had been when I met Nick.

The memory clicked into focus. "You were the guy Nick was talking to."

"Nick?" His face gave nothing away.

Oops, he'd been using John Smith at that point. "No, not Nick. I think it was John? Some guy I met there—he was talking to you, then I showed him how to find the entrance. He bought me a cup of coffee. But enough about him." I put my hand through his arm. "Tell me about yourself, Mr. Warenton."

The little man steered me along the gallery, making no effort to return to the busy center of the room. "There's not much to tell. Originally from Lewei. I run a mid-sized stone quarry and oxygen extractor here on Luna. I get back to the motherland about once a month, but I prefer Luna. The lower gravity is easier on my joints."

He paused beside a gruesome painting of what looked like the aftermath of a horror vid. Almost recognizable body parts lay strewn about a huge, blood-covered warehouse.

I looked away, wiping a film of sweat from my upper lip.

"Not a Jiangia fan?" Warenton chuckled. "She's definitely an acquired taste."

"Sorry, I wasn't feeling well earlier, and I think the pictures have triggered a relapse. Maybe I should find the ladies room again." I pulled my hand free, turning blindly away.

"Right here, Ms—what did you say your name was?"

"I didn't. It's Li. Katie Li."

"I thought so. Here you go, Katie Li." He opened a door and swung me through.

It snapped shut behind me, leaving me in darkness.

EPISODE 15: YOUR ONLY JOB WAS TO LOOK PRETTY

SERIOUSLY? Darkness again. What was with these people? "Hello?"

No one answered.

I tapped my Ncuff, illuminating the narrow hallway. Closed doors stood at regular intervals on either side, but the end was shrouded in shadow. I turned, but the door behind me had no visible handle or knob. I pounded my fist against the panel, then laid my ear to it.

Nothing.

"Fine." The word echoed weirdly along the hall. I stalked along the corridor, trying each door as I reached it. They all refused to open.

At the end, a set of steps dropped to a dim landing. I started down. My Ncuff went dark on the second step, leaving me in pitch black again.

Pushing back the panic, I tapped my device and continued to the landing. Another eight steps descended to another narrow landing. I hurried down.

This landing turned out to be a long hallway running perpendicular to the one above. Darkness enshrouded the left, but to the right, a light glowed under the third door.

Voices, muffled by the door, spoke. Someone shouted, but I couldn't understand the words. Then a hard thwack and a thud. I reached for the handle, my hand freezing on the cold knob.

What the heck are you doing Katie Li? It sounds like someone is getting beaten up in there—do you really think you should just blunder in?

But somehow, I knew Nick was inside and needed my help. That's why his friend, Mr. Warenton, had sent me here, right? Because Nick needed me.

Maybe you should let Mr. Warenton play the hero, Katie. He's a professional. Your only job was to hang on Nick's arm and look pretty.

Another internal voice countered. *Obviously, Mr. Warenton thinks you're an operative, too. And he thinks Nick needs an agent to get him out.*

Exactly! I told myself. *He needs an* agent. *Not a novelty salesgirl.*

Without conscious thought, my hand turned the doorknob, and the door opened on a scene that could have been portrayed in a Jiangia painting.

Nick looked up as I stepped inside. His ankles were secured to the chair in which he sat. His arms were behind his back, as if tied. Blood poured down his face, dripping onto his white shirt. One eye had started to swell.

Two burly men swung around to stare at me. They wore black clothes and identical expressions—which I would classify as "murderous." More blood left dark splotches on their T-shirts. The taller one swiped his arm across his face, leaving a smear of crimson on his forehead.

The shorter, wider man took a step forward. "Who are you?"

I froze, my mind blank. I had no idea what to say. There was nothing to keep these two men from taking me hostage and beating me into a companion painting for the Nick Beckett special. We'd hang in the gallery together, and Marjatta's wealthy friends would turn away in distaste.

"I'm Lady Lipinski's assistant." I spit out the first thing that came to mind. "She requires Mr. Beckett's presence upstairs immediately."

The two thugs exchanged a look, and the short one's eyes narrowed as he took another step toward me. "Lady Lipinski? What's she want him for?"

I lifted my chin. "That's none of our business. I don't ask why; I just do as I'm told. She wants him up in the office, now."

"They said we could—" the taller one began sullenly, but his companion cut him off.

"You heard the woman, get him out of the chair." He gestured to the hall. "We'll be right with you."

"You'd better hurry." I examined my fingernails with a bored sigh. "She doesn't want to miss Jiangia's discussion." I stepped back into the hall and let the door swing shut.

At the click of the latch, my heart and lungs went into overdrive. I clapped a hand over my mouth and nose, trying to prevent hyperventilation. "Oh crap, oh crap, oh crap."

Muffled voices emanated from the room again, cut off by more thuds and shouts. I reached for the doorknob again. Were the thugs ignoring me? Didn't they know Lady Lipinski was waiting?

I froze, my hand halfway to the door. What kind of crazy was going on in my head? Lady Lipinski was upstairs, oblivious to the torture occurring under her feet. Was my story so convincing I believed it myself?

And why would Marjatta's name galvanize these thugs into action? Was Marjatta involved in this somehow? I backed away from the door.

But what about Nick? They stopped when I went in. Maybe I could stop them again. I took a half-step forward, and the door pulled away from my reaching hand.

Nick stood before me, bloody but free. He grabbed both my arms by the elbow and swiveled me out of the way. Then he swung the door shut. He pulled a short rod from his pocket and pointed it at the doorknob. The knob started to glow, then heat radiated outward.

"That'll do it." He slid the rod into his pocket. "Good work."

"Do you have a sonic screw—"

He put bloody fingers against my mouth. "Not now. Come on. I'll try not to bleed on you." He urged me back toward the stairs.

"Good thing I'm wearing dark red." A giggle popped out of my mouth, and I slapped my hand over it, biting my lower lip to keep the hysteria at bay. I paused at the foot of the stairs. "The doors up there are all locked."

"We'll go this way." Nick nudged me into the dark hallway, stumbling against a wall. He grunted and clamped his arm around his waist.

I grabbed his arm. "Are you okay?"

"They might have broken a few things." He glanced at his side, then slung his left arm over my shoulders. "Most of the blood seems to be on the other side."

We limped along the dark hallway. "Do you know where we're going?"

"There should be an exit to the lower tunnels at the end of this hall." More of his weight sagged against me as we walked.

"How do you know where this corridor goes?" I slid my arm around his waist, and he jerked.

"Sorry, I think I've got a broken rib. Can you get my jacket? I dropped it."

I looked back. Light from the far end of the hallway illuminated a pile of fabric on the floor a couple of meters behind us. "Do you really need it?"

"It's an Arnami original. I can't wear these pants without it." He put a hand against the wall to steady himself as I stepped away.

"Tell the truth—your magic screwdriver is in the pocket." I stooped to grab the coat and turned to find Nick leaning heavily against the wall. "You need a doctor, now!" I wedged my shoulder under his left armpit and slid my arm carefully behind his back. "Where can I grab you?"

He laughed, the sound choked off with a hiss of pain. "Any other time, I'd have a different answer, but for now, how about you don't." His body stiffened as he gathered his strength, then he rolled forward, slumping heavily against me. "You can hold my belt, if that helps."

I wrapped my fingers through his belt loops on his right side and tried to support him without touching his ribs.

Footsteps thudded behind us—multiple people coming down the stairs, fast. I glanced over my shoulder, but no one was in sight yet.

"Stop." Nick's breath tickled my ear. He shifted me forward and turned us ninety degrees, so he could watch the hallway. "Gimme the jacket."

I held out the coat, and he slung it over his far shoulder, covering his bloodied white shirt. Then he pulled me close. "Your face is too pale—get behind the jacket. They shouldn't be able to see us in the dark. Be ready to run."

"Where?"

EPISODE 16: A CLEANING CLOSET MUST BE STERILE, RIGHT?

NICK TURNED his head and put his lips against my temple. "Don't move." His arm held me clamped to his side, his body tense against mine. I shivered as his hot breath tickled the inside of my ear. Leaning forward, I peeked under Nick's chin as the footsteps thudded louder.

Two men ran down the stairs, turning without hesitation away from us into the lighted end of the corridor.

"Move." Nick pushed me toward the door at the end of the hall.

Our shuffling steps echoed loudly in my straining ears. "Where does this door go?"

Behind us, someone swore. "Damn doorknob is melted."

"Go!" Nick put on an inhuman burst of speed, shoving me ahead of him as we barreled toward the end of the hall.

One of the goons pounded on the door. "What's going on in there?"

We pelted onward, Nick's breath now a ragged chant in my ear. "Go, go, go." He broke off with another hiss as we ran into the door at the end.

I scrabbled at the doorknob, sobbing in fear, my hands slick against the metal handle. My heart raced, the pounding blocking out the sounds of the goons yelling through the door at the other end of the hall. Then a soft click broke through, and the lights over our heads snapped on.

At the other end of the tunnel, a voice shouted.

I whimpered as the knob turned and was pulled away from my shaking hands. A brilliantly lit tunnel stretched away into the distance. Hidden behind the door, Warenton beckoned. "This way!"

I half-carried Nick through, stumbling against the rough lunar stone of the far side. The door slammed behind us, and something hummed. I twisted beneath Nick's shoulder, craning my neck, but only glimpsed Warenton sliding another thick, rod-shaped device into his inside jacket. "Where are we?"

Warenton ignored me. "That'll hold them for a few minutes. We need to get you cleaned up and back inside."

"What? Inside? No, Nick needs a doctor!"

Beside me, Nick leaned against the wall, his face gray and sweating, his eyes closed. I pressed my shaking fingers against his neck. His pulse was fast—was that good or bad?

"Nick?" Warenton's eyes darted to Nick's face, then back to me. "He's fine. Or he will be, in a minute." He picked up a case on the floor as someone slammed into the door behind him. Without a backward glance, he gestured down the tunnel. "Shall we?"

"Where are we going?" I pulled on Nick's belt loops, dragging him away from the wall. He stumbled against me, eyes still closed.

"Just a few more steps." Warenton stopped at a door marked "Maintenance" and produced a key. He slid it into the lock and clicked over.

We stepped into a dark closet, Nick's foot knocking into a docked cleaning robot—one of the big, industrial ones used on the inter-dome hallways. Nick's eyes popped open, and he spat out a word I didn't recognize. He dropped onto a box marked "towels, paper" and closed his eyes again.

Warenton pulled the door shut and turned on an overhead light. "Welcome to my temporary medical center."

"This is a cleaning closet." I flicked my fingers against an old-style push broom hanging from the wall.

Warenton grunted as he set his case on the vacu-bot and opened it. "Cleaning closet—must be sterile, right?" He pulled out a white box with a wide strap. "Roll up his sleeve, and help me get this on him."

I took the jacket still clutched in Nick's fingers and hung it over the top of the broom handle. Then I unfastened his cufflink, dropped it in my pocket for safekeeping, and rolled up the sleeve. "He said he has a broken rib." Trying to give Warenton room to work, I squeezed around him to Nick's other side.

The little ginger-haired man nodded. "That's usually what happens when someone tries to beat information out of you." He wrapped the strap around Nick's bicep and hit the button on the bottom of the plastek device. The screen lit up, and the device started humming. "This will diagnose and treat—to an extent. Your friends will break through any minute now. We should turn out the lights and be quiet."

The lights clicked off, and darkness dropped over us, mitigated only by the dim screen of the med scanner. Warenton fiddled with it, and it faded to black.

In the darkness, my hip pressed against Nick's shoulder. I slid my hand across his forehead, his skin damp and clammy against my fingers. I didn't know what I was expecting, or if cold and clammy was good or bad.

Nick jerked, then his arm wrapped around my legs. His hand, warm through the silky fabric of my dress, slid up my outer thigh and over my hip. It tightened around my waist, clamping me tight to his body. Muscles tensed.

Outside the door, footsteps thudded, then stopped. Beyond Nick, Warenton shifted, and something clanged softly, metal against metal. Our door handle rattled. I froze, holding my breath. Voices, muffled by the door, held a conversation, and the handle rattled again.

I didn't know who these goons were, but they'd beaten Nick and weren't likely to treat me any better. The sick feeling in my stomach swirled and grew. Cold sweat sprang out on my temples and upper lip. My ribs seemed to squeeze around my lungs, making breathing difficult.

Nick's arm tightened around my waist, then relaxed. He leaned his head against my side, his warm, even breath fluttering the fabric of my dress and sending tingles through me. The hurricane in my stomach settled to a slow swirl.

Beyond the door, the footsteps clattered away.

I touched the side of Nick's face. He turned his head, his breath warm as he made a faint shushing noise against my palm. I sucked in a deep breath, trying to bring my pounding heartrate down to normal.

Long minutes later, the muscles in the arm around my waist bunched. Nick seemed to tense, then rose, his arm sliding up my back and over my shoulder. "They're gone."

The light glowed on the med scan panel, illuminating the closet. Warenton, his face a sickly gray, pulled the device from Nick's arm. "Sorry about the noise. I think my belt buckle hit my briefcase latch."

Nick pulled his arm away, leaving me cold and bereft. He started unbuttoning his shirt. "You got a clean one?"

"Right here." Warenton pulled a folded garment from the briefcase and set it on the vacu-bot, then slapped a thin packet on top. "Clean the blood off your face before you go back in." He returned the med scan to the case, slammed it shut, leaving us in darkness.

The door opened, and light spilled in. Beside me, Nick wiped his face with his ruined shirt, light glinting on the brilliant crimson stains. The door slammed shut.

Fabric slithered against my bare arm, and Nick's hand knocked into my shoulder. "Sorry about that. Can you—?"

I tapped my Ncuff, illuminating the tiny room with a rosy glow. Light shifted across Nick's bare chest, muscles rippling as he pulled the clean shirt up over his shoulders. I licked my dry lips and looked away, my face heating.

"Can you help me with this?" A thread of laughter in his voice made my cheeks burn hotter.

"This" was a CleanWipe. I took the thin plastek packet and ripped it open with my teeth. "Where?" My voice was hoarse.

He put a finger under my chin, tipping my face up. I reluctantly met his eyes and he smiled, then pointed at his temple. The gushing blood had slowed to a mere trickle—probably an effect induced by the med scan—leaving a streak of red across his face.

I pulled out the wipe and started at the top, trying to imagine this was Harry or one of my coworkers, not a handsome, half-dressed secret agent. I dabbed at the edges of the split over his eyebrow, marveling at the speed with which the congealants had worked. "That must be a government grade med scan. Our kit at home doesn't work this fast."

"Harry gets into a lot of fights, does he?"

My eyes strayed to his brilliant blues, crinkling at the corners, and my face heated again. With an almost audible snap, I yanked my gaze back to the task at hand. "No, but he ran into a door a couple of weeks ago and ended up looking pretty much like you do now. I had to take him to the emergency room. He got five stitches." I folded the wipe and washed the blood off his cheek.

"Warenton left me a surgi-plast—it will do the trick while we finish the mission."

"Finish the mission?" My voice came out higher and louder than I intended. I swiped at the red on his chin and smoothed the cloth down his neck. The blood wiped away, leaving the fabric red and sticky. "You got another one of these?"

He handed me another pouch and took the sticky wipe from my fingers and dropped it on the floor. "Yes, we need to finish the mission. I've got enough drugs in me to keep me on my feet for another—" He looked at the chrono on his Ncuff. "Two hours, tops. I need to speak to my contact, meet your friend, then get back to my hotel before I crash."

"Can't someone else do it?" I clenched the damp wipe in my fist, staring up at him. "What if I don't get you home fast enough? I can't carry you."

His warm hands closed over my cold ones. "We'll get this done. I have faith in you. Am I clean enough to pass muster?"

I pulled my hands away. "If we were going to a mixed martial arts fight, yes." I pulled a mirror from my tiny purse and held it out. "Look for yourself."

He glanced into the glass, his hands busily buttoning the new shirt. "Once you get the surgi-plast on, I'll be fine."

"You have a black eye!" I did a double take. The swelling around his eye had gone down, the bruise fading to a more normal color. Now, he simply looked as if he hadn't gotten enough sleep. "What magic is this?"

He chuckled as he ripped open another small packet. "Modern medical miracles. Help me with this, will you? Stretch it just a bit as you stick it over the cut." He showed me how to pull the backing off the light brown oval of fabric.

I stuck the edge on his forehead above his cut, then stretched it as I pressed it against his eyebrow. The fabric tightened across the cut, then darkened a few shades to match his skin. "You're missing half an eyebrow, but otherwise I can't see the cut at all. That's remarkable. We should sell these at LCL."

"LCL? I thought you sold novelties." He looked in the mirror. "You got any makeup in that bag? Something you can draw an eyebrow with?"

I dug in my tiny purse. "Novelties are just one of the businesses under the LCL umbrella. If you get good at sales, they bump you up to the medical sales team. I'm pretty sure they don't have those." I jerked my chin at him as I pulled items out of my bag. "Blush, lipstick…it'll have to be the mascara." I twisted the end and pulled out the brush.

He grabbed my wrist as I raised my hand. "Thank you." Our eyes met and held for a long moment, then he let me go. "Go easy. Less is better."

"Tell that to Zendas." I coated the end of a stylus in mascara and used it to draw the suggestion of an eyebrow on the surgi-plast. While I was there, I brushed a little powder over the remaining bruise on his cheek. After a moment, I stepped back and compared my work to his other brow. "It'll do at a distance. But if anyone looks carefully—"

"I'll stay away from everyone." He nodded and handed the mirror back to me. "It's good enough that no one is going to remember if I had it before or not. That's the key."

"I thought you wanted to meet Marjatta?" I slid my cosmetics back into my bag and snapped it shut. "She'll notice."

He shrugged into his jacket, wincing as shoved his arms into the sleeves. "You can tell her I ran into a door this morning. How do I look?"

I turned up the brightness on my Ncuff and looked him over, shaking my head in disbelief. "No one should look that good after what you went through. I didn't look this put together when I arrived tonight!"

He straightened the onyx pin at his throat and smiled. "You looked fantastic. Still do." He tapped my cheek with his index finger, and little tendrils of warmth curled through my body in response. "Put out the light."

I tapped my Ncuff, plunging us into the now familiar darkness.

EPISODE 17: WHAT IS YOUR DEFINITION OF DANGEROUS?

I REACHED out and put a hand against his chest. "You're burning up."

He clasped a hot hand over my cold fingers. "I'm fine. The stimulants from the med scan ramp up the system—including temperature. I need to get the job done and find a place to collapse before they wear off."

"You need to get to a doctor." I took a deep breath, not believing I was actually going to suggest this. "Maybe *I* can meet with your contact."

Nick laughed, and his hand tightened on mine before he let go. "Thanks for the offer, but they wouldn't talk to you. It took me weeks to get this set up. It has to be me."

Relief washed over me, almost taking my breath away. "Are you sure?"

"Yes. But I'll keep that in mind for next time."

Next time?

At the end of his last mission, he'd said we'd never meet again. And yet, here we were. I was thrilled by the idea of continuing our partnership. I'd been terrified tonight—more than once—but working with Nick Beckett was exciting. And let's face it, despite my continued reminders to myself that he was just using me as cover; that he'd disappear into the night and I'd never see him again; that he was a secret agent and I was just...ordinary—despite all that, I was halfway in love with him.

He leaned close and put his mouth to my ear. I shivered—I would never not get a thrill from that. "I'm going to open the door. Step back and stay quiet. If anything happens, stay in here—I'll draw them away."

"No!" I breathed the word out, but he didn't hear. Or he ignored me. His arm came out, pressing me deeper into the tiny closet. Then the doorknob turned, and light spilled in through the crack between the door and jamb.

We froze, listening, but all I could hear was the blood thrumming in my ears.

Nick opened the door a little farther and darted into the hallway. I gnawed my lip, waiting for what felt like hours.

"Clear." The door swung wide, and Nick held out a hand.

I took a shaky breath and put my hand in his. "Let's go."

The door into the Varian was locked, but Nick pulled a key from his pocket and unlocked it. "Warenton left me this."

"Who is he?" I followed him into the hall, keeping my voice to a low whisper.

"Later." His finger tapped my lips, and he moved away down the dark corridor.

The hall was empty. The room where they'd held Nick was locked. What had happened in there? I told myself that my appearance had given him a will to live and an opportunity to surprise his captors, but maybe they'd let him go because I said Lady Lipinski wanted him.

If that was the case, why did they chase us? And why would Marjatta's name work that kind of magic? I made a mental note to ask later. We crept up the steps and through the dim hallway. The door at the end, leading back to the gallery was closed. Nick stopped and straightened his jacket. He cocked his elbow at me. "Ready?"

I took a deep breath, gripping Nick's arm tightly.

He reached across and pried my fingers from his arm. "You're putting holes through my sleeve." He stroked my cold hand and laid it back in the crook of his arm. "Showtime."

We stepped into the gallery. As before, people filled the central area, but they all faced away from us. A high-pitched voice carried over the murmuring crowd, no doubt assisted by expensive audio equipment.

"…the monolithic composition is counterbalanced by the abstract…"

I tuned her out. "It's all blood and gore, if you ask me."

As Nick steered me to the left, angling toward the nearest column, he spared a glance at the closest painting. His footsteps faltered, and he did an exaggerated double-take at the huge canvas. "Not my preferred style." He leaned close and dropped his voice, his whisper tingling in my ear. "I'm going to leave you here for a few minutes. Mingle. If anyone asks about me, I'm just over there." He nodded at the crowd.

I clutched his arm. "What if you don't make it back?"

He patted my fingers. "This isn't dangerous. I'll be back in a few."

"You were just abducted by thugs and beaten to within an inch of your life. What is your definition of dangerous?"

"That wasn't related to this mission." He lifted my hand to his lips like a character in a period drama and raised his voice to normal speaking level. "I'll get you a drink. You look parched."

I stared after him, my fingers tingling where his lips had touched. If life were normal, I'd be swooning and daydreaming and writing "Katie Beckett" in my notebook. I gave myself a quick mental shake. *You have one job, Katie— distract the enemy. Whoever they are.*

I meandered through the crowd, cautiously inserting myself between whispering art-lovers, as Jiangia yammered on and on about light and inspiration. I caught a man staring at my cleavage, stared back until I caught his eye, then channeled Marjatta's mother to give him my best death glare. He went pale and turned away, muttering something to his companion as he excused himself.

I turned away and looked down. Crap. I'd missed a spot of Nick's blood on my chest. I pulled a tissue from my bag and swiped at the quickly drying splotch. A little spit should do the– "What?" I hissed at another staring bystander. "You've never seen a woman cleaning blood splatter off her boob before?"

As a server swung past with a tray of half-empty glasses, I dropped the bloody tissue on it. Growling at guests and wiping blood from my chest in public was probably not the best way to maintain a low profile. I took a drink from another passing server and pretended to listen to the artist.

If the thugs who'd kidnapped Nick weren't related to this mission, then why had they taken him? Should I go find him now in case he needed rescuing again? I smirked to myself. Imagine me, Katie Li, purveyor of cheap baubles and joke novelties, rescuing a secret agent. But that's exactly what had happened.

A round of applause brought me back to the present. The crowd thinned as guests scattered to look at paintings or sneak away to other less-prestigious events. I sipped my drink, careful not to swallow more than a mouthful or two. I didn't need to get drunk twice in one evening, even if the first time was not my fault.

Marjatta swept to a stop beside me, a handful of men and women swirling around her. I watched the others carefully, wondering if one of these had been the one who'd stung me.

"Where's your date?" Marjatta held out a hand, and someone put a glass into it. She sipped and held it away. "Too sweet. Can you get me something drier?" A man standing nearby snatched the glass out of her hand and turned away, looking for a server.

"He's over there." I waved my bag vaguely beyond her entourage. "Getting me a drink."

"You have a drink." Marjatta took my glass and sniffed, then handed it off again without looking. "That's terrible."

"I didn't have one when he left." I watched as a woman in a green dress glared at me, then spirited my glass away.

"And now you don't again. Perfect." Marjatta's eyes traveled around the room, then zeroed in on someone behind me. "And if I'm not very much mistaken, here he is."

I turned as Nick approached. He handed me a glass with a half-bow. "As requested. Long, cool, and alcohol-free."

A couple of Marjatta's minions snickered. I ignored them and took the glass. "Thank you. Nick, there's someone I'd like you to meet. Lady Marjatta Lipinski, this is Nick Beckett. Nick, this is Lady Marjatta."

Nick smiled his thousand-watt smile and bowed, taking Marjatta's hand. "What an honor to meet you."

Marjatta smirked. "I'm sure it is, but we've met before, Nick. Or should I call you 'John?'"

EPISODE 18: I DON'T DO ANYTHING HALF-WAY

"JOHN?" Nick looked from Marjatta to me, a faintly amused expression on his face. "I don't get the reference. Am I supposed to be a paid escort or something?"

Marjatta stepped forward and poked Nick's chest. "You introduced yourself as John at Katie's party. Why are you Nick now?"

Nick blinked, then chuckled. "I didn't think you'd remember anything from that night. You were—" He glanced at the entourage surrounding us. "You were having a good time."

"I was wasted." She smirked and waved, encompassing everyone in the gallery in her vague gesture. "They've all seen me party before. I don't do anything half-way." She slid her hand through Nick's arm and turned him around to walk beside her. "Tell me about yourself."

Nick grabbed my hand, pulling me along. "I'd love to get to know you better, Lady Marjatta, but Katie and I have another engagement."

Marjatta's eyes widened, and she stopped suddenly, grinning like a crazy woman. "By all means, don't let me detain you." She pulled her hand away and made shooing motions. "You two kids go have fun." She winked.

My face went hot at the implication. "It's not—"

"I really am sorry to have to cut this so short." Nick tapped his Ncuff. "May I send you my contact information? I'd like to take you out for coffee—perhaps tomorrow?"

Marjatta nodded and tapped her own device to accept the data. "We'll schedule a time. But only if Katie comes, too." She eyed me. "Before you go, let me borrow her for a second. A quick trip to the ladies' room." Not waiting for his reply, she grabbed my arm and hustled me across the room.

The women in her entourage followed, their heels clattering almost in sync against the fine lunar stone floor. Marjatta paused at the door and turned to stare at them. "We'll be right back."

The brunette in the green dress opened her mouth, but her companions shushed her. She glared mutinously at a friend, then gave Marjatta a phony smile. "We'll wait here."

"Are you trying to get me drugged again?" I hissed as the door shut behind us.

"What are you talking about?" Marjatta sailed across the room to the mirror I'd used earlier that evening. Hard to believe it had only been a couple of hours ago.

I turned, showing her the pink circle on the back of my arm. "One of your lovely friends hit me with a stinger at your parents' house. I don't know why, but those wenches are cut-throat."

"Oh, honey, I'm sorry. I'll have someone find out who did that. It is not okay."

I waved her off. "Don't worry about it. But don't expect me to show up for any more of your society events. I'd rather keep our friendship on the down-low."

She snickered at my outmoded slang. "Now that you've been seen with me —and that tasty specimen out there—I'm not sure you'll be able to stay under the radar anymore. But I can get you some anti-stinger. I take it before every event."

"Are you serious? Those things are used so much you have to prep for it?"

An exaggerated look of superiority crossed her face. "It's a common date-rape drug. A smart girl is prepared. It never occurred to me you wouldn't— sorry, that was uncalled for. I wasn't trying to call you stupid. I get so catty around those girls." She made big eyes at me and held out her arms for a hug. "Do you forgive me?"

I wrapped my arms around her. "You live in different circles than I do! I can't be mad at you for trying to protect me. But I gotta go."

"What's the hurry?" She grinned and shook her head. "Don't answer that. Speaking of protection, you have some, right?" She wiggled her eyebrows, then opened her tiny purse. "Hang on, I have—"

"Marjatta! I just met the guy!"

"You met him at Milo's." She started ticking events off on her fingers. "Then he came to your party. And he bought you pastries the next day. By my count, this is your fourth date. And you've known him for weeks. You're overdue."

"Meeting at Milo's wasn't a date. And he's been dirtside for weeks, not here, getting to know me."

"Third date then." She dug through her bag. "Right on schedule."

I grabbed her hand. "No. That's not going to be necessary."

She looked up, cocking her head as she stared at me. Then she nodded. "Good plan. Make him wait. I'll expect a full report tomorrow morning. And I'm serious. If he shows up for coffee without you—tomorrow or any other day —I'm out. He doesn't seem like the type to kiss up to you just to get to me, but—"

My heart dropped. That's exactly the type he was—except he'd been completely upfront about it. I summoned a brilliant smile. "He told me he wanted to meet you. He said it was business-related."

"Really?" Marjatta's eyebrows drew down. "That's odd. Unless he's using *me* to get to my parents."

I shrugged and glanced at my chrono. Crap, I needed to get Nick out of here. "I need to go—I don't want to keep him waiting so long he gives up on me."

She waited for me to open the door for her. It was one of those automatic, subconscious moves that unintentionally reinforced the differences in our social status. In a place like this, it didn't bother me. I knew I was out of my depth. I pulled the door. "After you, my lady."

The flock of socialites swirled around us, deftly cutting me out in the process, and flittered away with Marjatta at their center. She looked over her shoulder at me and rolled her eyes. Green Dress glared before lifting her nose and turning her back. That one needed remedial training in the art of the icy snub—she definitely had plenty of opportunities to practice.

I gave a little finger wave, although none of them saw it. Then I scanned the crowd for a tall, handsome Norse god. Although with the short, dark hair, he now looked more "military hero" than "Thor."

"Going my way?" Nick poked his elbow at me. His eyes were brilliant, and a damp sheen covered his face.

I touched his burning hand. "We need to get you out of here." I slid my arm through his and guided him around the perimeter of the room toward the door. "Where am I taking you?"

"I have a room at the Seasons. Why isn't it the Four Seasons? That's what it's called on every other planet." His voice took on the sing-songy quality of the inebriated.

"Because this is a moon, and we don't have real seasons. Besides, it's not owned by the same company. Everything in Luna City is owned locally. It's the law." I pushed through the first set of double doors and into the lobby. "Paris Dome, right?"

Nick tapped his Ncuff. "Got a map right here—'n case I get lost. These domes are confusing." His screen lit, and he tapped an icon. The words "where am I staying" scrolled across the Ncuff, then a map appeared with three different routes marked. Nick squinted at the screen, staggering into me. "Walk, mini-cab, or train? It's a beautiful night. Shall we walk?"

"It's the same night it always is on Luna, and you're in no state to walk. We'll take the train." I steered him toward the drop chute. Was he drunk or acting? Or maybe it was the meds. "Down two floors to the A line."

We stepped into the drop chute, and Nick staggered against the wall, grabbing my hips for balance. "Oops, sorry, didn't mean to muss your dress." His hands slid around my waist, pulling me close. "That's better. You smell good."

I leaned back, putting my hands flat against his chest. "You're feverish. And possibly delirious. Don't do anything you'll regret later.

His bright eyes roamed over my face. "I won't regret anything later. You're really pretty. Can I kiss you?"

I longed to say yes. The heat pouring off his body soaked into mine, leaving me relaxed and sleepy—exactly how I imagined a day on a beach would feel, but without the sand and bugs.

My bones turned to jelly, and the hands pushing him away slid across his muscular shoulders without thought. My brain screamed at me to stop, that this was just the fever talking, that Nick was just using me for cover, and there was no hope of a happily ever after. But my heart refused to listen. I sighed and melted against him.

EPISODE 19: YOU SMELL LIKE MY MOM

THUD.

We stumbled. Nick let go of me, and I grabbed the wall for support, looking around in surprise.

We'd hit the bottom of the drop chute. "I've never been down this far." I stepped out of the chute, Nick following close behind.

We stood in a long, gray hallway. Thick conduits hung from the low ceiling overhead, and an unpolished lunar stone floor stretched away in a long, graceful curve. I checked the sign near the drop chute. "I think this is a maintenance corridor. We shouldn't have been able to go below the station."

Nick's arms snaked around me again, pulling me against him. "Good, no one here to interrupt us."

I turned in his arms to put a hand against his forehead. "We really need to get you some medical attention. Do you have anything at your hotel, or should I take you straight to the clinic?"

He pulled away. "No clinics!"

"We could tell them you got beaten up by random thugs." We didn't have a lot of crime in Luna City, but if a tourist wandered into the wrong part of Boston or Sydney domes, they sometimes got into trouble before the police noticed and tracked them down. "Wait a minute. The authorities can track us by our Ncuffs. Location, vital signs—they track tourists very carefully—it's bad publicity to have them apprehended or injured by locals. Why didn't they come rescue you back at the Varian?"

Nick nuzzled against my neck. "Turned off the tracking. Can't have them watching us." His hands slid up my back, burning through the thin dress.

I grabbed his shoulders and pushed him away. "Do you have medical care at your hotel?" I enunciated each word clearly.

"Of course. We should go. I need a nap." He sagged against me.

Perfect. From randy to exhausted in the flicker of an eye. I pushed him back into the drop chute and tapped the "up" icon. We rose a level and staggered out into the train station.

This was the A train—the one that served the wealthier domes, like Hua Hin, Paris, and Beijing. The station was sparkling, almost sterile. White tile shone in the yellowish lights, and soft music played over the speakers hidden in the overhead. In the far wall, four pairs of heavy airlock doors hid the train tracks. It was still early, and the event in the Varian was in full swing, so the station was deserted.

I eased Nick onto a bench against the wall and sat beside him. His head drooped to my shoulder. "You smell good."

"I know, you said that before. It must be the hairspray Francois hit me with."

He rubbed his cheek against my shoulder. "'s nice. Like my mom."

I turned to stare at the top of his dark head. Five seconds ago, he was trying to kiss me. Now— "I smell like your mother?" The words came out loud and half-hysterical.

He jerked upright. "What? No. I meant—I dunno what I meant. Definitely not like my mom." He gave a little shake, as if trying to jog the pieces into place. "I don't know why I said that." The red faded a bit from his face. "Must be the fever talking."

I put my hand against his forehead. Like a mom would. I tried to not roll my eyes. "You feel cooler. Maybe the medication Warenton gave you just needed more time to work. I thought it was supposed to wear off, not go the other way."

Nick dropped his elbows to his knees and hid his face in his hands. "I think it might be two different things. The stimulant was supposed to keep me going for two hours. The other stuff was supposed to fight infection and help with the healing. Right now, I feel like—" He put his hands on the bench and shoved himself to his feet. "If I sit too long, I'm going to pass out."

With a soft hiss, the airlock doors opened, revealing the interior of the A train. Comfortable seats, two to a side, faced forward, with another pair facing back to create little four-person pods. I wrapped my arm around Nick's waist and pushed him into the train. He winced and stumbled against me, then dropped into one of the rear-facing chairs.

He patted the seat between himself and the train wall. "Sit here. Otherwise, I might fall over, and I'm not sure I can get back up." The words came out reluctantly, as if admitting to that weakness took a supreme effort of will.

I dropped into the seat and looped his arm over my shoulders. "It's a short ride. You can trust me to get you home."

His eyes sagged, and his leaned his head against the back of the seat. "Thanks, Katie. I knew you were a good choice. Sorry about the mom thing. And—" He opened his eyes a fraction. "Sorry about getting…overly friendly. I know you don't want that."

He clearly doesn't know anything.

I stared past him at the window as the train whooshed away from the station. In the reflection, I could see pain etching a deep groove between Nick's eyebrows. I turned toward him, wanting to smooth away the mark and the pain causing it.

Hand halfway to his face, I froze. I needed to be smart about this whole relationship, not emotional. And by relationship, I meant spy-business-partnership, not personal relationship. I knew myself, and I knew it would be way too easy to fall head-over-heels for this guy, then spend the next year-and-a-half crying after he disappeared. I was already half-way gone, and we'd only met four times.

Get a grip on yourself, Katie. Keep it professional. I let my hand drop back into my lap, then nudged Nick with my elbow. "Next stop."

Somehow, we got out of the train and into the drop chute. Nick's Ncuff allowed us access to the Season's fourteenth floor, and we stepped into a wide corridor with thick carpet and tasteful wallpaper. I staggered down the hall, Nick draped over my shoulders. Half-carrying, half-dragging him, I stopped at each door and waved his arm at the access plate. The fifth one on the right opened, and we tumbled inside. I kicked the door shut behind me and dropped him on the huge bed.

A dim light by the door provided enough illumination to see him sprawled there. "Nick, we're here. Where's your med kit?" I shook his arm.

He rolled his head away, eyes closed, and let out a deep sigh.

"Nick, where's your medical gear?" I shook a little harder.

He flapped his hand at me as if batting a fly and muttered something under his breath.

I went to the bathroom and soaked a washcloth in tepid water. While I wrung it out, I looked in the mirror. My dramatic updo had devolved into a messy roll. Fortunately, messy was all the rage—I'd seen at least three women at the Varian with similar hairstyles. My eyeliner was smudged, and a faint streak of dried blood still decorated my collarbone. I swiped at it with the washcloth, then rinsed and went back to Nick.

He snorted once, softly, as I approached. A little puddle of drool decorated the bedspread by his cheek. Not exactly the image of a sexy secret agent now. Even so, my heart went into double time when I gazed at his face—relaxed and so young looking. I'd assumed he was in his late twenties or early thirties—

surely secret agent school took longer than regular college? But now he looked about seventeen.

A really hot seventeen—bulked up, soon-to-be-recruited-by-the-pros, grav-ball star seventeen.

After draping the damp cloth over his forehead, I crossed to the suitcase standing against the wall. I put the expensive-looking gray case on the folding stand and checked the external pockets.

Nothing. The large inside compartment was empty, too. Time to rifle through the drawers.

I peeked under the damp cloth to make sure his eyes were still closed, then faced the three-drawer cabinet. It felt wrong to go through a man's drawers when he was asleep—like something out of a romantic suspense vid. What if I found a bloody knife and a butchered rabbit?

The woman in the mirror over the bureau looked pale, with huge eyes and a tremor in the hand I pointed at her. *Snap out of it, Katie! You're an agent—at least for now. Act like one.*

I pulled open the top drawer. A stack of T-shirts took up one side. The other held four neatly folded rectangles of silky material. Curious, I pulled one out. The packet unfolded into a pair of gray and black striped boxer shorts.

"You like them?"

EPISODE 20: GOOD MORNING, ROBO-WENCH

I SPUN AROUND, my face burning, the silky boxer shorts clutched to my chest. Nick had lifted the bottom of the washcloth, and peered at me from beneath it, grinning. My mouth opened and closed, but nothing came out.

He chuckled and let the cloth fall across his eyes. "The med kit is in the second drawer. White bag with a green star."

I clenched my teeth and turned back to the dresser, shoving the boxers back into the drawer and slamming it shut. I *was* going to refold them until he laughed at me.

The white, rectangular case sat next to what appeared to be pajama pants in a yellow duck print. I grabbed both from the drawer and returned to the bed. "Let's get you doped up, and then you can put your jammies on." That last bit might have come out a little snarky.

Nick dragged the cloth from his face with a slow hand, his lips twitching. "Girls seem to like the duckies." His hand dropped to the bed with an almost soundless groan.

I sucked in a breath and opened the white case. He was injured, and I was treating him like a—I wasn't sure what. Like I didn't care about his suffering, for sure.

Of course, he *was* a bit smug.

I pulled the device from the case. This med scan looked almost identical to the one Warenton had used—standard clinic issue. It was unusual for a private citizen to have one but not unheard-of—especially someone embarking on a visit to a different planet. Or in this case, moon. If the advertisements were to be believed, prepared travelers—and hypochondriacs—around the galaxy carried them as a matter of course.

I started to roll up his sleeve again.

He struggled to sit up. "Help me get this shirt off before I pass out." He'd already unbuttoned the front, and in the dim light, his smooth skin and hard abs were clearly visible. I swallowed, hard, then moved around the bed to his side where his chest wouldn't be in my direct line of sight.

When I pulled the sleeve off his arm, I got an eyeful of his bare shoulder and broad, muscular back. I focused on the med scan, breathing deep in an effort to slow my pulse rate. I got the thing wrapped around his arm without drooling on it—or him—which I considered a success. Then I hit the "go" button and backed away.

He slumped to the bed, his face gray and his eyes closed. A damp sheen covered his skin. He was really ill, and he needed my help.

Contrite, I jumped forward. "Why don't you move farther up the bed, so you can sleep." I helped him shift until his feet no longer hung off the end. "I'll take your...shoes off."

A quick grin slid over his face and disappeared.

While the med scan hummed, I pulled his shoes off and tucked him under the covers. If I were a better med-tech, I'd have helped him remove his pants, but that was way outside my comfort zone.

To be fair, I'd had a long, stressful night. Getting drugged at the Lipinski house. Finding Nick and confronting a pair of goons in the process of beating him. Hiding from said goons. Completing the mission while tolerating Marjatta's smug friends. Trying to fight off the amorous advances of a feverish secret agent.

Admittedly, I hadn't tried too hard.

Single-handedly returning the injured agent to his hotel, then treating his injuries. Not to mention the long day at work and enduring Francois.

Considering all that, I was practically a hero.

I tucked the covers around Nick's bare shoulders, then sank beside him on the bed. I'd close my eyes for a minute while the med scan did its thing, then—once I knew he was out of the woods—I'd go home.

———

Simulated sunlight peeked through the gap between the curtains. I rolled over, throwing an arm over my eyes.

We couldn't see the sun in Luna City—except in the Hills, with its transparent domes. And due to our tidally locked orbit around Lewei, the real sunrise and sunset did not coincide with the established beginning and ending of the day. At all.

Most of the domes had simulated daylight, with the overhead lights shifting from dim to bright across the dome from east to west. At "night," the overhead lights went out, and lights on the buildings provided illumination.

If you were lucky enough to have a window, you could wake up to simulated sunrise every morning.

I didn't have a window in my bedroom.

I pulled the arm from my face and sat up.

I was alone in Nick's hotel room. The covers had been pulled over my elegant evening gown, now crushed and creased. A smear of makeup on the pillow made me glad I couldn't see the mirror from there. I averted my eyes as I stumbled to the bathroom.

Luckily, it was empty. I locked the door behind me and snapped on the lights. Ugh.

Water drops glinted on the glass shower door. Apparently, Nick had already washed and dressed. He must be fully recovered. Maybe he went to get me coffee. For a few seconds, I debated the wisdom of using a man's shower, but the lingering scent of lemongrass and rosemary decided me.

After a quick shower with the most amazing bodywash and shampoo, I toweled off and slid back into my crumpled dress. The steam from the shower had helped with the worst of the creases, but I'd still look like the morning-after walk of shame to anyone who saw me creeping home. I ran the hotel-branded comb through my wavy hair and took a deep breath. Time to face the music.

Except there wasn't any.

Now that my eyes were fully open, it was obvious Nick was gone—completely gone. His suitcase was missing, as were the T-shirts and boxers.

Yes, I checked.

The med scan was also missing. The neatly folded pajama pants and a new T-shirt, still wrapped in plastek, lay on the dresser. On top, there was a sheet of hotel notepaper with a single, hand-scrawled word: thanks.

I opened the plastek and shook out the shirt. It was a women's medium—perfect for me—and pink, with a big yellow duck on the chest.

Blinking my inexplicably stinging eyes—I must have gotten some of that lemongrass shampoo in them—I slid out of the red dress and pulled on the shirt and matching pants. The drawstring tightened enough to keep them from sliding down my stick-like hips. I folded the bottoms up a few centimeters, and the fabric held a cuff better than I expected. A tap on my Ncuff matched my ballet flats to the shirt. I shoved the dress into the hotel-provided laundry bag, took a quick look around to make sure I hadn't forgotten anything, and slunk out of the room.

A small package wrapped in HotKrisp paper sat on a tray outside the door. Still blinking furiously, I stooped and picked it up. The deep-fried cinnamon made my eyes water more. I sniffed and read the receipt—charged to John Smith.

Clutching my dress and my beignets, I hurried to the drop chute, wiping my damp cheeks on my shoulders.

———

It was still obscenely early, so I saw no one I knew as I returned to my apartment. Since Hummy was on night-time mode, she didn't announce my arrival. She merely blinked my name across her screen in a self-righteous font.

Good morning to you, too, robo-wench.

The couch and both armchairs were occupied. A pizza box containing only crusts covered most of the coffee table. Harry and two friends snored in a dissonant concert as the hologram of a woman with improbably large breasts and ridiculously tiny armor surveyed the room, her chest rising and falling in exaggerated detail.

"Sorry, Zeena." I shut down the game and tiptoed into my room.

Once inside my sanctuary, I locked the door and slid down to sit against it. The coffee I'd picked up at the truck outside the hotel steamed gently in a KeepWarm cup. I opened the HotKrisp wrapper and spread it across my lap to enjoy my breakfast in solitary splendor.

Fortified by way too much fried pastry, I disposed of the evidence and slunk out of the room to wash the last of the tears from my face. Then I returned to the bedroom and dumped my dress out of the plastek laundry bag. I held it up by the hem and shook it. With luck, the creases would come out in the Fabri-Cleane.

Something clinked on the floor. I tossed the dress onto the bed and crouched to retrieve a small, gold item—Nick's cufflink.

Why did I have it? I ran a hand through my now dry and slightly frizzy hair as I tried to recall the details. That whole part of the night was hazy—as if my brain couldn't cope with reality and had decided to make the scary parts more dream-like.

I threw myself on the bed beside the dress, staring up at the ceiling. I'd taken the cufflink off his shirt when we did the first med scan in the maintenance closet and stashed it in my pocket.

Incidentally, the pockets on that dress were one of the reasons I loved it. Not only were they convenient for storing small items, but they were located in such a way as to enhance one's figure—depending on the shape of item stored there. You wouldn't want to carry, for example, a rectangular tin of mints.

I checked said pockets for the other cufflink, even though I didn't remember taking the second one. In fact, I was relatively certain he'd removed that one himself when he changed into the shirt Warenton had brought.

Which reminded me—he never did explain who Warenton was. Obviously, a local contact—but maybe not as local as me. He hadn't known the Hills could be a dangerous place to discuss secrets.

I flipped onto my stomach and tapped my Ncuff. The city directory might shed some light on Mr. Warenton. I typed in his name and waited while the NexUs churned through its databanks and returned an answer. At eight on a Sunday morning, the net speeds should be pretty fast.

My Ncuff pinged, and I tapped the results. An Albirt Warenton lived in Paris Dome. Nope, too old. I scrolled through the entries, discarding one after another. Finally, an Endral Warenton appeared. I tapped the name and brought up the entry. Address in Sydney—one of the lower cost domes. And a link to more information.

A list of articles appeared—apparently, his son Daniel Warenton was a well-known high-school athlete—or he had been fifteen years ago. I tapped an article, and a picture of three boys standing on a winners' stand appeared.

The one on the left looked exactly like a young Nick Beckett.

EPISODE 21: YOU TOLD ME, GENIUS

WHAT THE HECK? Nick had grown up in Luna City? That couldn't be right. He didn't know enough about—well, about anything here.

Or did he? He'd known about the warren of tunnels under the Varian Center—something I hadn't known, and I'd lived there since I was four. Maybe his tourist persona was just a cover story. But his muscles meant he spent a lot of time on Lewei.

None of it made sense. If I could find this article, it would be dead easy for an enemy espionage unit. He had been posing as a wealthy businessman from Lewei, not a local boy made good. This article would call his identity into question. I would have thought the LIA would do a better job of providing a consistent cover story.

I put a cold hand against my forehead, trying to stop the new throbbing in my skull.

My Ncuff pinged—an event had been added to my calendar by Marjatta: "Coffee with Katie and Nick." Scheduled for next Friday morning at ten.

I sent a text to Marjatta: **Did you just invite me for coffee?**

She replied: **Nick called and set it up. Where are you?**

Me: **Home. When did he call?**

Marjatta: **You went back to your place? Why didn't you go to his hotel? Nothing against your apartment, but it's not as nice as the Seasons.**

Me: **Who said we went anywhere together? And how did you know he was staying at the Seasons?**

Marjatta: **You told me, genius. Why don't you come over here? I have pastries.**

I closed my eyes, my stomach protesting the idea of more pastry.

Me: **I'll be over after my workout.**

Marjatta: **Can't you skip it—just this once?**

Me: **Nope.**

I signed off and changed into my exercise gear.

The lower gravity on Luna meant residents lost muscle mass over time. If you never intended to leave Luna, it didn't matter. Marjatta's family had been Lunites for generations, and she had no intention of ever going dirtside. Plus, if she did, she was wealthy enough to stay in a low-g hotel and hire low-g transportation. She'd only have to endure the higher gravity when she went into one of the historic buildings, and a specially fitted (read expensive) grav belt could help with that.

I, on the other hand, was not wealthy. And besides, I wanted to travel. If I was going to go all the way to Lewei—or Gagarin, or maybe even Armstrong —I wanted to be able to go where I pleased. At the age of seven, I'd declared my intention to see the galaxy, and my parents had signed me up for the Extra-Lunar Ambassador program. They knew better than I that physical fitness was only part of the equation.

The Luna City government tightly controlled who was allowed to enter and leave. In order to be granted a travel visa, a Lunite must not only be physically fit but also had to meet certain other requirements. One of those was graduation from the Ambassador program.

The program brought me into contact with other kids from all over Luna and trained us to be the best possible ambassadors for our moon. Over the years, the need for daily physical training had been burned into my psyche. So, I went to the gym every day, preparing for the time I'd be ready to—

Wow, that sounded really smug and kind of brainwashy.

Short story: I worked out religiously, so I could travel someday.

———

Marjatta and I hung out on Sunday afternoon, but she had no idea where Nick had called her from—or if he was even still on Luna.

I worked all week, selling more whoopee cushions than I cared to talk about. Apparently, news of the anonymous delivery to the premier's home had sparked a surge of copycat orders. We shipped cases of the things to addresses all over the Leweian empire.

Some of those people might even have been happy to get them.

On Friday morning, I called in sick. I thought about skipping Nick's meeting with Marjatta, but she'd said she wouldn't open the door if he was alone. Not that she opened her own door, but I got the point.

I also wasn't sure what Nick's intentions were toward Marjatta, and I wasn't going to let him take advantage of her.

My decision to go had nothing to do with wanting to see him again. Because I didn't.

I folded the duckie pants and stuck them into the laundry bag I'd taken from the Seasons. I debated adding the T-shirt, but there was no way it fit him. And it was really cute.

When I arrived at Marjatta's, Kerdin opened the door. "Good morning, Citizen Li. It is very nice to see you again. Lady Marjatta is expecting you."

"Hey, Kerd! What's going down?" I pumped out my fist to see if he'd bump it. Sometimes, I imagined Kerdin was one of those high-tech androids from a science fiction novel, and I tried to confuse his programming. He was usually ready for me.

He surprised me by knocking his knuckles against mine, then he bowed again. "All is well, Citizen." His face remained passive, but the corners of his eyes crinkled just a tiny bit.

I flung open Marjatta's sitting room door. "I made Kerdin smile."

Marjatta looked up from her book. "You did not. He's not programmed for that."

I'd told Marjatta my "theory" a long time ago.

"I did. His eyes crinkled, just a little. It was glorious." I flung myself down on a chair beside the couch. "Is he here yet?"

"Kerdin? You just saw him." She tossed the reader on a side table.

I gave her my best stink eye. "No, not Kerdin."

"It's nine-thirty. The meeting is at ten."

"Good point. You got any snacks? My workout was brutal today."

She tapped her Ncuff and ordered something from the house system. "You called in sick, but you still worked out? What if your employer checks your gym record?"

"Prentice wouldn't do that—I never abuse my sick days. Besides, everyone knows how dedicated I am—can you imagine me skipping the gym, without being on my death bed?"

The door opened, and a small box rolled into the room. It stopped by Marjatta, and the top popped open. She reached inside and pulled out a flask of water and a plate of cookies. "High-protein cookies—your favorite."

I snagged a cookie and poured myself some water. "Your house makes the best cookies."

"I'll be sure to tell the Auto-chef."

At precisely ten o'clock, someone knocked twice on the door. It swung open without waiting for an answer, and Kerdin announced, "Lewei Citizen Nicholas Beckett."

Nick strode into the room, nodding thanks to Kerdin as he passed. "Lady Marjatta, so nice to see you again. And Katie, you look well."

Marjatta rose and the two of them did the air kiss thing. I got to my feet and let Nick take my hands. "I brought your duck pants back," I blurted.

His eyes lit up, and he chuckled. "My duck pants?"

I gestured to the flat packet on the side table. "Yeah, you know, the ones I borrowed." My face went hot, and out of the corner of my eye, I caught Marjatta staring at me. I opened my mouth to explain, then decided that would only make matters worse.

He sat next to Marjatta. "You could have kept them, but thanks. They're my favorites."

My face burned hotter as he turned to Marjatta. The two of them did the small-talk thing, discussing common acquaintances and recent events they'd attended. Apparently, he'd been on Luna several times since we first met. Part of me was upset he hadn't gotten in touch, but I reminded myself this was business. Spy business.

Who knew spy business could be so boring?

Strange that they had so many contacts in common, and yet he'd needed me to make the introduction. Maybe it was all fake? He'd probably looked up Marjatta's public calendar and cross-referenced it to other probable attendees. Claiming casual acquaintance meant he didn't need to know much about them.

Exactly ten minutes after ten, Kerdin arrived with coffee and pastries. Marjatta poured, and we all sipped. I felt like I'd strayed into one of those historical vids.

They chatted some more—nothing that sounded significant to me, at all. Both of them attempted to draw me into the conversation, but since they were talking about people I didn't know—and had no interest in—I was not much help.

After thirty minutes, Nick rose. He bowed to Marjatta, thanking her for a lovely morning, and picked up the duck pants. Then he turned to me. "May I see you home?"

I glanced at Marjatta.

"I've got another engagement at eleven, Katie, but let's get together this weekend, shall we?" She sounded like a bored socialite, then she ruined it by adding, "You can tell me about the duck pants."

My face went hot again. "Sure. I'll see you later." I followed Nick to the door.

We took the drop chute to the first floor and walked to the inter-dome tunnels. "That was uncomfortable. Did you get what you came for?"

"I just wanted to meet your friend." Nick pulled my hand through his arm, rolling his eyes at the ceiling as he did. "She was delightful, as expected."

I did a double take. Was he worried about being overheard? I could play along. "Yeah, totally chill and fun."

We walked in silence for a few minutes. When we reached the Hub, I stopped. "You don't need to go all the way to Boston with me. But I wanna know about this." I pulled up the picture I'd found of him. "Is that you?"

He stared at the picture on my Ncuff, clearly calculating what he should say. After a moment, he smiled. "It was. I can't believe the LIA left that picture up. My cover is blown."

"You don't seem too upset about it. Especially since this ties you to Luna City. You're supposed to be a visiting Leweian. This says you grew up here."

"Look again—that was an intra-system event. I was competing for Lewei. The kid in the red shorts was the local."

"Daniel Warenton. That's how I found the picture—I searched on Warenton."

His eyes flickered, and I could practically see him sorting and discarding options. He went on the attack. "You looked up Warenton?"

I nodded. "You wouldn't tell me who he was, and I wanted to know. He clearly doesn't know about the sound problems in the Hills, which makes me think he's not a local."

Nick's eyes narrowed. "He is a local, but you're right about the Hills. He should know better. Which makes *me* think he wanted us to be overheard. How did he know you'd be there?"

"He couldn't. I didn't know I'd be there."

"You said yourself it was a strange coincidence. Do you go to the Hills regularly? Maybe it's something you always do after a party?"

I frowned, thinking. "I guess it is, but how would he know that about me? I didn't even realize. And why would he care about me? I'm a random girl you met at Milo's."

"That's what I thought, too. Maybe I was wrong."

EPISODE 22: WHY ARE YOU LYING?

"YOU THINK HE SET US UP?" Nick and I walked across the Hub and into the Beijing tunnel, speaking in low tones. The feet and voices of scores of passing Lunites should have prevented eavesdropping even if we were yelling, but better safe than sorry. "Did Warenton want you to meet me? It's true I always shop at Milo's, but he had no way of knowing I'd be there."

"You were shopping for a party—who knew about it?"

"It was a party—everyone knew about it." I gave him an exasperated look. "All my friends, all Harry's friends—heck, even the old people at his job probably knew about it. He tells them everything."

"What old people?"

"Harry works at a retirement community. Shouldn't you know that?" I looked around, surprised to notice we'd almost reached Mother Frane's tent. "You got any change?"

Nick fished in his pocket and pulled out a five-credit bill. "That's the smallest I've got."

I snatched it from his grasp. "That'll work." I pushed the paper into Mother Frane's cup and looked under the edge of her tent flap. "Good morning, Mother."

"Katie, so good to see you. And your off-world friend is here again." She gazed up at Nick, her eyes unfocused at such a distance. "Come closer."

I moved to the side and knelt on the mat beneath the tent flap. Nick crouched beside me. "Nice to see you, Mother."

The old woman smiled and patted his cheek. "You're a nice boy." Then her eyes narrowed, and her thin eyebrows drew together, as if she'd noticed something odd. "Why are you lying to Katie?"

His eyes darted to me, then back to the old woman. "Lying? What would I be lying about?"

"I don't know, but you should come clean. She's a steadfast friend, but you need to be honest with her."

Nick laughed and straightened up. "I'll keep that in mind."

As I rose, Mother Frane pointed her bent finger at me. "Be careful, Katie. I've been around a long time."

"I know, Mother." I kissed her cheek and started to back out of the tent. Then I paused. "Have you always lived in Luna City?"

The old woman nodded. "My whole life."

I glanced back at Nick, then scooted forward. "Do you recognize this boy?" I pulled up the picture I'd shown Nick earlier.

Mother Frane drew in a sharp breath. "That's him." Her blurry eyes travelled from me to Nick and back, and she tapped her bent finger on the screen of my Ncuff. "And this boy—Daniel Warenton died not long after this."

"Died? I didn't see anything about a death when I searched."

'They covered it up. I heard he was someplace he shouldn't have been, and he might have gotten mixed up with the wrong crowd. Powerful people can get away with terrible things."

Nick dropped to one knee again and lowered his voice. "You think he was killed by the mob?"

Mother Frane pulled back the edge of her tent to look up and down the tunnel. A constant stream of Lunites moved in both directions, none of them paying attention to us. "There's no mob on Luna. That's a myth." Her laugh came out hard and unconvincing.

"Can you tell us anything about this boy or his family?" Nick asked.

The old woman shook her head. "No. It's not safe. They aren't safe, and now, neither are you."

"What do you mean?" I asked.

Nick held up one finger, then pulled a couple of twenties from his wallet. "These are the only small bills I have. Thanks for the information. I owe you."

"Take care of our Katie." Mother Frane tucked the credits among her layers of clothing. "That's all I ask." She leaned forward and gave me a swift hug. With her lips close to my ear, she whispered, "He's lying to you, but I trust him."

I pulled back and nodded at her. "Thanks for… thanks."

Nick pulled me to my feet, and we continued down the tunnel.

When he didn't speak, I glanced at him. "What did you make of all that?"

He patted my hand, safely lodged in the crook of his elbow again, and shook his head the tiniest amount. "How did you become friends with her?"

Had he asked because it was important or to stop me from talking about Warenton? With a mental shrug, I told him. "You know I grew up here. Moved to Luna when I was a child. My dad and I used to walk through here. He didn't like the trains and only rode them when Mom was with us. One day, some teens were hassling Mother Frane, and Dad ran them off. From then on, we always stopped to say hello when we walked through."

He nodded absently but didn't ask any more questions, so we walked on in silence. When we reached my door, I stopped and turned to him.

Nick spoke before I could say anything. "May I come in?"

"I—sure." I waved my Ncuff at the door, and we went inside.

When we reached my apartment, he walked over to Hummy and stared at it. "How about you show me your bedroom."

I hesitated. "You've seen it before."

"Yes, but the whole place was full of people. I'd like a more *intimate* tour." His low, sexy voice contradicted his serious expression and the tiny jerk of his eyes toward Hummy.

"Oh, right." My voice came out high and unconvincing. If anyone was listening to us through Hummy, they'd know something was up. Or that I was a nervous wreck when a man asked to see my bedroom. Which was probably more convincing than if I'd hammed it up.

I pushed the door open and gestured. "There it is."

Nick rolled his eyes as he took my elbow and urged me through the door. "Why don't you lock it—we don't want to be disturbed."

As I activated the lock, I cleared my throat and tried to bring my voice back into the audio range real people could hear. "Harry won't be home until five anyway."

"No more talking." Nick sat on the bed and patted the mattress beside him. "Come here."

I gulped and sat down on the far end of the bed.

He activated his Ncuff, then reached into his pocket and handed me something. Earbuds.

I threw a confused look at him, but he put a pair of them into his own ears. "How about some music?" It was his voice, but his lips hadn't moved.

A female voice said, "Mm hmmm," and a popular Leo DeVoss song started pulsing through the room.

Then my Ncuff vibrated.

An unknown contact. I jerked and threw Nick a panicky, questioning look.

He pointed at my Ncuff and mouthed, "Answer it." He pointed to the earbuds in my palm.

As I inserted the first one, the murmurs and sighs started.

Nick reached over and tapped my NexUS, and a call connected. "Sorry about this, but it's the best I can do for now. Put in the other earbud. Unless you enjoy listening to... you know." His eyes sparkled, but a tinge of pink washed over his cheeks.

I scrambled to get the other bud into my ear, but not before I heard my own voice murmur, "Oh, Nick."

My face went nuclear hot.

"Don't talk." Nick's voice came through the earbuds, soft but clear. His lips barely moved as he spoke. "Years of practice." His lips twisted at my raised eyebrows. "You were going to ask me how I can talk without making any sound."

He was right. I waved for him to go on.

"Based on what Mother Frane said, I think we have to assume Warenton isn't necessarily on our side. He's never mentioned his son, and the coincidence of you being in the Hills that morning is suspicious. He's lived here too long to not know about the weird sound bouncing. We should assume he wanted to bring you into this, but I don't know why. Why you? You aren't a trained agent."

He stopped talking, and his eyes narrowed. "Are you? Now's the time to come clean."

I shook my head violently.

After a long scrutiny, he nodded.

Although the earbuds masked external sounds while he was talking, when he fell silent, they got through. My whole body went hot, then cold when a voice—I'd swear it was mine—made an inappropriate suggestion.

Nick had the grace to blush for real that time. "Sorry. I had that recording built from samples of your voice—it's terrifyingly accurate. Where was I? Oh, yeah, Warenton. We need to figure out why he picked you. What's special about you? No, don't answer. Just think about it. We'll find a safer place to talk later."

He turned the music up, sending it through the call to drown out the recording. Then he slipped off his shoes, pulled his feet onto the bed into a cross-legged position and closed his eyes.

I stared at him in disbelief. Who can meditate to Leo DeVoss? I hummed along with the music, waiting for the recording to end.

EPISODE 23: MAYBE IT WAS ALIENS

A BIT LATER, Nick's voice cut through the music. "It's almost over. I have a better meeting place in mind, but I need to sweep it before we can talk there. My software will modify the—" His face went pink, and he grinned sheepishly. "—the *audio* so it isn't an exact repeat. We can use it again, but only in *appropriate* locations."

I pressed my cold hands to my cheeks. Even though I didn't hear most of the recording, I got enough to start my imagination running on high steam. I swallowed and nodded.

"I can see it's not comfortable for you, so we'll try to keep it to a minimum." His own cheeks were a bit flushed—maybe I wasn't the only one feeling the heat.

"I need to do some investigation—I'm going to head out. I'll give you a call this week." He slid his feet back into his shoes and stood.

I pulled the device from my ear—the music still played in the background, but there were no other sounds. Perfect. My lips twitched as I asked, "You're just leaving?"

"I gotta go, sweetness."

I gave him the stink eye. "Sweetness?"

"You don't like pet names?" He grinned as he swiped through his Ncuff, and the music faded completely.

"I don't like generic pet names. You can do better than that." I made a face at him.

"You're right, I'm sure I can come up with something more appropriate for you." He leaned forward and before I could react, kissed me on the cheek. "I'll call you." Then he was gone.

Love 'em and leave 'em seemed to be the name of the game in the spy world. My cheeks blazed again at how appropriate that phrase would be to anyone listening.

Then my eyes narrowed. How would they be listening? And who? When we first arrived, Nick implied he didn't trust Hummy, our apartment's HumanChat module. But there were no Hummy pickups in my bedroom. I'd insisted on that before I moved in.

But Nick didn't know that. Was I safe here? Or was he concerned someone had planted a listening device in my room. Or—yikes—on my body?!

It could have happened while I was out cold in the ladies' room at the Varian Center. Were subdermal listening devices a thing? Surely that was science fiction, not reality?

But who knew what the Commonwealth could produce? Official news outlets claimed their technology was all stolen from us, but the rumors said otherwise. I'd heard about miniature holographic Ncuffs that you could wear on a finger and audio implants. Listening devices implanted under the skin didn't seem that farfetched.

Maybe it was aliens!

Okay, now you're getting hysterical.

Hysterical or not, I needed to know. I locked my door and stripped off my clothing, examining myself in my small mirror. If the device was small, any signs of the implantation could have healed by now, but I should still find a lump or something.

After a few minutes, I gave up. Nick had said he knew of a place we could talk safely, and he knew way more about all this spy gear than me. As long as I didn't say anything dangerous, I was safe enough.

I got dressed and sat on my bed. What was dangerous?

———

Marjatta called that afternoon, demanding an explanation for the duck pants. She wouldn't relent, so I met her for dinner and gave her the sanitized version. I could tell she didn't believe I'd just slept there, and of course I couldn't tell her about Nick's injury.

"He'd had too much to drink. He's almost as much of a lightweight as a Lunite, believe it or not. When we got back to his hotel, he passed out."

"What about this morning? Where did you two go after you left me?"

I took a deep breath, trying not to blush.

She pointed at me. "You didn't do it Saturday night, but you did today!"

"No! He just walked me home. And kissed my cheek. That's all." I picked up my glass and gulped down some water.

She gave me a narrow-eyed glare, then shrugged and picked up her chopsticks. "I believe you. You don't look like a woman who had a quickie this morning. Way too tense. Besides, I know you'd tell me if you did."

———

By Thursday, I was starting to think Nick had disappeared from my life. He hadn't called. I'd rescued him from thugs, gotten him to medical attention without alerting the authorities, and returned his duck pants, and to thank me he made me sit through a half-hour of simulated intimacy, then disappeared.

When my comm pinged, I knew it was him. There's no way I could have known, and I'd taken eighteen calls that morning. But I knew.

"Greetings! You have reached Luna City, LTD. Your call may be monitored for training purposes. My name is—"

"Hi, Katie, remember me?" Nick grinned from the screen.

"You probably shouldn't call me here." I glanced around the room, but no one was paying any attention to my caller. "Unless you're going to buy something?"

"As a matter of fact, I am. I need three cases of fried chicken candy."

I scrolled through the catalog and found the little yellow tins. "Three cases? Are you having a party?"

"The boss likes to give away gag gifts at our quarterly meetings. He loved the rubber chickens but thought candy would be both funny and appreciated."

"You know it tastes like fried chicken, right? It doesn't look like chicken."

"Are you trying to make a sale or prevent one? You gotta work the upsell, Katie. You should be offering me mashed potato taffy to go with it." He laughed.

"Unfortunately, we don't carry that. I'll make a note to recommend it to our purchasing agent." I rolled my eyes at him.

"That's more like it. Now, I want this delivered to..." He reeled off an address.

My software automatically entered it into the system and pulled up a cross-check. "You're having it delivered to the Seasons in Port Royale? Your company quarterly meeting is on Luna?"

"It's a stockholder meeting." He shrugged. "They like to show the big guys some love by flying them to interesting locations."

I logged into his account, and the system populated the billing information. "Are you charging it to the account on file?"

"Yes, ma'am!" He smiled. "Maybe I'll get a chance to drop by Luna City and see you again?"

"That would be fun." I finished the order and sent it to his screen for approval. "When's the big event?"

"Next weekend. I'll let you know if I can get away. Or maybe you can meet me in Port Royale?"

"I've never been there before." I clicked on the screen and submitted the order. "Will there be anything else, Mr. Beckett?"

"No, thank you. I hope to see you soon, Ms. Li." He winked, and the call ended.

I wished I knew what I was supposed to know. Apparently, Nick and I were now friends, and it was okay for everyone to know that? And was I really supposed to go to Port Royale?

Two days later, that question was answered. A virtual ticket to Port Royale appeared in my email, with a note from Nick. "See you Friday."

EPISODE 24: MEET ME AT MOTHER'S

"WHAT ARE you going to do in Port Royale?" Marjatta picked up a shirt from my bed and tossed it at me. "Not that one."

"This is one of my favorite shirts!" I folded the faded pink fabric and slid it back into a drawer.

"And it looks like it. You need classy clothing for a guy like Nick." She turned away from the bed and riffled through the closet again, shaking her head. "I need to send over a few things. Will you promise to take them?"

I crossed my fingers behind my back and nodded.

"You don't mean it. That's okay, I can work with that." She tapped her Ncuff and scrolled through a few screens. "On the way."

"What do you mean?"

"I've got someone sending a few things over. They'll be here in twenty minutes."

I plopped onto the bed and leaned against the headboard. "You live in a totally different world from me."

"I know." She picked up the pink T-shirt with the duck. "What's the story with this shirt? I haven't seen it before."

"Do you have my wardrobe memorized?" I snatched the shirt from her and folded it carefully.

"No, but you returned some duck pants to Nick at my house. I didn't think you were big into ducks."

I shrugged one shoulder. "They're nice. And we don't have them on Luna."

"Exactly." She pointed at me. "Nick gave you that shirt, didn't he?" She

107

snatched it up again and turned it inside out to display the print on the side seam. "See! Made on Lewei. Not Luna."

"I'm sure you can buy duck shirts on Luna. Maybe they're imported." Nick left that shirt for me the morning after our visit to the Varian Center. It was too small for him, so I'd assumed he'd picked it up in the Seasons gift shop. Maybe the pants, too—although those had been in his drawer when we arrived. Surely, he didn't bring me a shirt from Lewei? How would he have known I'd need it?

The answer to that question sent a cold wave through my body. He *expected* me to spend the night with him. He couldn't have known he'd be injured, but he'd assumed I'd need a shirt the next morning. Either that, or he always carried a women's T-shirt with him.

Come to think of it, he'd said something about girls liking the ducks. It also explained why he'd been so amused when I brought the pants back. He probably carried them all the time—just in case a woman needed them. What a thoughtful date.

Yuck.

I took the shirt and tossed it into the dirty clothes bin. "Never mind. I don't want to take it after all."

"If he gave it to you, it would—"

"No!" I dropped against the headboard. "In fact, I'm having second thoughts about this whole trip."

"Don't do that. Go. Have a good time. He's a fun guy. Just don't expect too much." She sat on the bed beside me. "Dating doesn't have to be serious."

"Yeah, I know," I mumbled as I turned away.

"This is what you don't do." She pointed a finger at me. "Don't get all emotional and crushy. If you're falling for him, it's time to back away. He's not the serious type. I don't want you to get hurt. Maybe you shouldn't go."

She was right. Unfortunately, there was more to this relationship than a relationship. He invited me to Port Royale because he needed my help with a mission. But I couldn't tell her that. I took a deep breath. "It will be fine. I'll go and have a good time and come home refreshed and relaxed. No strings attached, no hard feelings when it ends."

She gave me a long, hard look. "If you're sure…"

My Ncuff vibrated, and a message from Hummy appeared. "A package has been delivered."

"That was fast." I got to my feet and trudged down the hall. When I opened the door, a woman stood there, not the bot or abandoned box I'd expected. She wore a white coverall with red and blue stripes down one side and the letters LCE on the chest. "I have a package for Katie Li. ID, please."

I flicked the identity button on my Ncuff, and it sent a signal to the woman's device. She nodded as the transmission appeared, then picked up a large box and thrust it at me. "Have a nice evening."

I swung the door closed, holding the light parcel. "You messengered clothes to me?"

Marjatta met me at the door to my room. "Sure. It was much faster than going home and getting them myself." She took the box and ripped the EZ-Open tab across the top.

As she unpacked the box, I looked at my closet and half-open drawers. I couldn't imagine directing someone to the specific clothing item I wanted and telling them to pack it.

A satisfied noise from Marjatta brought my head round. She held a white corset against her body. "This is perfect."

"I'm going to Port Royale, not a lingerie party."

"Those aren't mutually exclusive. And private lingerie parties are the best."

I heaved a sigh. She was determined to set me up for a weekend lovers' retreat. "Thanks. Throw it in."

"You don't throw clothing like this." She lovingly laid it into my duffle bag. "I should have had them send better luggage, too."

———

I stepped off the train in the Paris Dome. Every city on Luna had the same layout and the same names. Each city was built of the same standardized parts, and some genius decided it would be easier for travelers if everything was set up exactly the same. So, Port Royale had the same domes and trains as Luna City.

The businesses in each dome weren't always identical, but the bigger companies stuck to the plan. The Seasons hotel was always in Paris, and the Varian Dome always housed the *Honor and Glory to the People of Lewei Hall.*

This Paris was just enough different to be disorienting. I ignored the strange signs and businesses and made my way to the Seasons Hotel. On the inside, it was identical to the Luna City hotel, except for the words Port Royale across the bottom of the check-in desk. I moved to the deserted desk, looking for a bell to ring.

There wasn't one, but a uniformed man appeared as if by magic. Or as if summoned by a motion detector. He beamed a professional smile in my general direction, one that said he didn't think I was worth his time.

"Welcome to the Seasons. May I help you?"

I waved my Ncuff over the sensor imbedded in the desk and opened my mouth. Before I could say anything, the smile changed, and he met my eyes. "Citizen Li, thank you for joining us! Your room is ready, and I've transferred the access code to your Ncuff. Razine will show you to your room."

As I stared at him, open-mouthed at the sudden efficiency, someone tried to pull my duffle bag from my shoulder. I spun around to confront a man with a name tag reading Razine. It was Nick.

Stunned, I stood rooted in place as he took my bag and started across the lobby. After a few steps, I ran to catch up with him. "What are you doing?"

He kept walking. "Please, Citizen, follow me to the drop chutes." We rode without speaking and exited on the seventh floor. "Room 723."

What was he up to? I thought we were meeting for a romantic getaway—or at least the appearance of one. Why was he pretending to be a bellboy? Maybe he *was* a bellboy. Maybe this whole secret agent thing was a setup—some kind of prank.

No, the beating he took at the Varian looked real enough. *But was it?*

I shook my head. No one would go to this much trouble to prank me.

At the room, I waved my Ncuff at the access panel, and the door unlocked. Nick pushed it open, then held it for me. I gave him a narrow-eyed look as I passed, then plopped onto the bed.

"Here's your bag, Citizen." He set it on the bed beside me and held out a hand.

Did he expect me to tip him? I pulled a couple of Lunatics out of my pocket and dropped them in his palm. He gave me a professional nod, his eyes cutting to the bag. Then he left.

I stared at the closed door for a few seconds, then stood. The room was paid for—that had better include the mini bar. I yanked open the small cooler and pulled out a candy bar and a soda. Then I opened my duffle bag.

I moved my clothing to the dresser, one piece at a time. Tucked between two shirts, I found a note. How had he managed to get that inside my bag during our short trip from the front desk? Or had someone else slipped it in earlier? The bag had been in the overhead compartment of the inter-dome train. Maybe one of my fellow passengers had slipped it in. But in that case, there was no reason for Nick to play bellhop.

I picked up the folded paper and opened it to see four words in blocky print: Meet me at Mother's.

EPISODE 25: THOSE ROBOT ARMS AREN'T GOING TO HURT ME... I HOPE

MEET ME AT MOTHER'S? The only mother Nick and I had in common was Mother Frane, but she was in Luna City. I had to assume the note meant to meet him in the tunnel between Beijing and the Hub. But when?

My Ncuff vibrated. A calendar reminder appeared on the screen: dinner at six o'clock. No further information. I would assume that answered the question of when to meet. That gave me two hours to enjoy the Seasons.

My stay was being charged to Nick's expense account—how in Lewei did he manage that without an obvious link between us? I shrugged and pulled up the roster of services. Not my problem. I connected to the Sylvan Spa.

A woman in a white lab-style coat answered my call and booked me a sixty-minute massage and therapeutic soak. "Bill it to my room," I said in my best Lady Marjatta voice.

The Sylvan Spa occupied the entire top level of the hotel. I took the drop chute up and stepped into a jungle of potted plants. Tinkly music played in the background over the sound of a dripping fountain. I pushed through the fronds of an oversized fern, the musty, green scent wrapping around me.

Beyond the fern, the room opened out into a kind of grotto, with water trickling down a rough stone wall on the left, and more exotic foliage around the edges. Huge blossoms hung from every plant, and the scents of jasmine and vanilla nearly overwhelmed me.

A woman seated at a small table stood. "Welcome to Sylvan Spa. You must be Citizen Li." She held out a thin metal plate.

I waved my Ncuff over the plate, and a light on the bottom edge turned green, confirming my identity. The woman nodded and pressed a button. A section of the wall hinged away, taking the plants with it and revealing a hallway painted a warm off-white. "Your room is the open door on the left. Enjoy your visit."

I smiled nervously and hurried down the hall. An attendant waited inside, dressed in flowing white pants and a shirt that fit snugly over her upper body. Her dark hair was tied back in a low tail. "Welcome to the spa, Citizen Li. Please disrobe and lie on the table, face down. Your massage therapist will be with you shortly. Do you have any questions?"

When I shook my head, she left.

I hung my clothes behind the decorative screen, then climbed onto the bed and pulled the sheet over me. Heat emanated from the table, making me drowsy. I'd never had a massage before, but Marjatta raved about them. And the Seasons was renowned for their spa services.

I'd just started to drift off when a gentle chime bonged through the room. The lights lowered, and a click sounded overhead. I lifted my head out of the donut-shaped face thing and cranked my neck around. My breath caught in my throat. Doors had swung open in the ceiling above me. Four robotic arms extended, each bearing a life-like hand on the end. Two of them grasped my feet, one touched my right shoulder, and the last one gently grasped the back of my head.

"Please lie face-down," a low, mellow voice said as the hand tipped my head back into the donut. Like I had a choice.

What had I gotten myself into?

Don't panic. People rave about the Seasons' spa. Wealthy citizens from all over the system use their services. These robot arms aren't going to hurt me.

My body did not agree with this assessment. Every muscled tensed—as soon as that thing let go of my head, I was going to spring off the table and bolt for my clothes.

The hand holding my head didn't let go. But once the other three started kneading, I didn't care anymore. They dispensed a thin layer of massage oil on my skin, then worked my muscles with exactly the right pressure. At some point, the fourth hand released my skull, but I barely registered it. From time to time, the voice asked me if the pressure was right, or if I was warm enough. I wasn't sure I made a coherent answer.

When the massage finished, the voice told me to lie there as long as I liked. "When you're ready, you can move to the soaking tub." The hands tweaked the sheet into place and retracted into the ceiling.

After a few minutes, I sat up and looked around. The wall to my left had retracted, revealing a deep tub. More of the plants from the lobby hung over the gently steaming water, and the scent of jasmine had returned, less overwhelming this time. I pulled the sheet around me as I slid off the table and padded to the changing area. My Ncuff said I still had half an hour before I had to meet Nick, so I abandoned the sheet and slid into the bath.

My Ncuff buzzed, startling me out of my hot tub induced stupor. If it had been within reach, I might have slapped it off and ignored it, but I'd left it across the room, and it kept buzzing. I heaved a sigh and climbed out of the bath.

Ten minutes later, I approached the drop chute, warm, relaxed, and sleepy. I soldiered past the allure of my room—a nap sounded perfect right now—and took the chute to the tunnel level. The walk from Paris to the Hub and out to Beijing would take at least ten minutes, but I was too relaxed to care about being late.

There were no homeless people living in the tunnels here. Was that because Port Royale provided housing for everyone or because they shipped the less fortunate somewhere else? Based on what I'd heard from Mother Frane, I guessed the latter.

Like in Luna City, very few pedestrians walked the tunnels. Ahead of me, a group of rowdy young men joked and pushed each other around as they made their way to Beijing. An older couple gave them a wide berth, then strolled past me, headed for the Hub. Without the tents along the walls, I had no reason to loiter in the middle of the tunnel. I slowed my steps and strolled along, pausing to tie my shoe and check behind me. The couple had disappeared into the busier Hub. I straightened. The young men disappeared into Beijing. I increased my speed and reached the center of the tunnel.

A door opened in the wall as I drew level, revealing a dark tunnel. I looked both ways to make sure I wasn't being watched, then darted inside. The door shut, leaving me in a dimly lit hallway. Thin light strips glowed along the edges of the ceiling and floor, leading me forward. There were no doors, so my path was obvious.

I trudged up the hallway, trying to forget that, the last time I'd wandered alone in dark corridors, it had resulted in finding Nick being beaten. But that wouldn't happen this time—Nick was the one who'd sent me here. Of course, last time, it had been his co-conspirator, Warenton. Maybe not a good sign.

I was going to need another massage when this was done.

I rounded a corner, and light poured from an open door. Squinting against the glare, I stepped into the room.

"You're late." Nick's voice was flat and unfriendly.

I blinked quickly to let my eyes adjust and turned to take in my surroundings. The room looked like an office—desk, comm system, white board with sticky notes tacked to it, dusty shelves stacked with odds and ends. But who has an office at the end of a creepy tunnel in the bowels of a lunar city?

Nick leaned against the shelves to the left, his arms crossed over his chest. Behind the desk, a short woman sat, her posture equally unwelcoming. Without the ever-present nail polish and highly teased blonde flip, I almost didn't recognize Betzy.

EPISODE 26: GET THE DOOR, PHOENIX

"BETZY?" I stared at the short woman. She looked completely different. Partly because she was in an office hidden in a dark tunnel under Port Royale rather than ignoring calls at the LCL office, and partly because she wasn't painting her nails or chewing gum. Her usually poufy blonde bob was slicked back against her head, giving her a serious demeanor.

She sat forward, leaning her elbows on the metal desk. "Katie."

Nick straightened up and moved around the desk to stand beside Betzy. "Suppose you tell us what's going on."

I stared from one to the other, my mind a blank. "I have no idea. You sent me a ticket to Port Royale and left a note in my duffel bag. I thought you wanted me here."

"That's not what I'm talking about—I know I did those things. I want to know who you are and why you got into the middle of my network."

"And *how* you got into the middle." Betzy drummed her jewel-toned nails against the desk. The sound echoed loudly down the hall. "Get the door, Phoenix."

Nick moved around the desk, his eyes never leaving me. He pulled the door closed and locked it with a loud snick. Eyes still burning into me, he side-stepped to his original place against the wall.

I licked my dry lips. "I don't know what you're talking about. I'm here because Nick sent me the ticket."

Betzy's fingers stilled, and she pointed a royal blue claw at me. "How did you get inserted into this network? Who do you work for?"

At least the last question made sense. "I work for Luna City, Limited, just like you, Betzy. You know me—we've been working together for two years."

The blonde pressed her fingers above her eye, as if she was getting a headache. "I know you work for LCL. What agency do you work for? Lewei? Colonial? Gagarin?"

"What? No! I told Nick—I don't work for any agency. I just work for LCL. I got involved in all this when Nick left those mints in my Milo's order." I swung around to look at Nick. "Tell her—I'm nobody."

His brows came down. "You really don't work for anyone?"

"Phoenix," Betzy snapped.

The name finally sank into my consciousness. Nick's code name was Lunar Phoenix. "Are you LIA?"

Betzy did a double-take, then her eyes narrowed. "You know I can neither confirm nor deny that."

I put my frozen fingers against my cheeks, trying to get my brain in gear, but nothing made sense. "I'm not LIA or Colonial or Gagarian. I'm Katie Li from Luna City, Limited, and I sell whoopie cushions for a living." My cheeks burned—it was humiliating to admit that was the total sum of my existence. "I'm not a spy. I'm not even very good at helping spies."

"That's not true." Nick stepped toward me, one hand reaching out as if to touch my arm. He glanced at Betzy and pulled back. "You did a fine job of patching me up. And you introduced me to Lady Lipinski."

"That could have been a setup." Betzy picked at her lower lip. "Why would the opposition want you to meet Lady Lipinski?"

Nick spread his fingers. "I'm supposed to be working into the network on Luna. Maybe she's part of that network."

Betzy held up a hand. "Enough—"

I broke in. "You think Marjatta works for the Colonials? Or Gagarin? That can't be true! She grew up on Luna, just like me. We're loyal citizens!"

"I'm sure that's what everyone is supposed to believe. And it's possibly true." Betzy grimaced at Nick. "It's up to you. Do you think we can turn this around?"

He shrugged. "We don't know what we're trying to turn. But I think I can unravel it. And Katie is either completely innocent or a magnificent actor."

"I'm not an actor—I get stage fright."

They both glared at me for a second, then ignored me again.

Betzy drummed her nails a few more times—making me want to scream—then slapped her hands on the table. "Fine. Keep her on a tight leash. Report any discrepancies to me. And don't spill anything." She waited until Nick nodded, then pushed back from the desk and got to her feet.

As she passed me, she pointed two fingers at me. "I'm watching you."

I wrinkled my nose and pointed two shaking fingers back at her. "Okay."

When she left, Nick closed the door behind her. He turned, a faint smile on his face. He pointed two fingers at his own eyes, then at me. "This is supposed to be intimidating. It means I'm watching you."

I hunched my shoulders. "I didn't know. I figured it was some spy thing."

He chuckled. "No. Let's get out of here."

I grabbed his arm as he reached for the door. "Can't you tell me what's going on? Why was Betzy here? Why does she hate me? Who is Warenton, really? Why—"

"Whoa, one question at a time. Betzy is my contact in Luna City. Warenton is a local—he has unofficial ties to the Lewei government and possibly the mob."

I gasped. "The—I don't want anything to do with the mob! You know they run Luna City?"

"They pretty much run every city on Luna. And they try to run the government. Which is why I'm infiltrating—it's a balancing act."

"You think Warenton put us together—that he told you to go to Milo's at the time when I would be there, so we'd meet? But why?"

Nick leaned against the desk. "That's just a guess. He hasn't admitted to setting up that accidental meeting, but the fact that you were in the Hills the next morning just when we were talking—he clearly wanted someone to overhear our conversation. He'd never be sloppy enough to talk secrets in a place that's known to have acoustical anomalies. It's still possible you were just a coincidence—in both places."

"But you don't believe that." It wasn't a question.

"No, I don't. Warenton was supposed to help me meet another agent—Betzy. I think he confused the two of you and…" He lifted both hands as he shrugged.

I didn't like being considered an accident, but it kind of made sense. "So, Betzy doesn't hate me—she's just mad because I got in the way?"

"Yeah. But you've been an asset, and I'd like to continue working with you —if you don't mind." He gave me a sheepish smile. "You're already here."

"Why *am* I here?" I gave him my best icy glare.

"I told you—having a friend on Luna gives me an excuse to come up here. And you can be my plus one when I need one—couples look less suspicious."

"Like at the Varian—someone to distract the watchers?"

He straightened and stepped forward, putting his hands on my upper arms. "Exactly. And you're fun. Nothing wrong with having a little fun."

Warmth from his hands seeped into my arms and spread through my body, combatting the chill of the room—and the situation. "I'm not going to end up on the lunar plain with a low air tank and a holey suit, am I?" I'd heard how the mob handled betrayal and not just in the entertainment vids.

He held up one hand, palm out, and put the other over his heart. "I'll always be there with a spare tank and patch kit."

The chill returned, but I appreciated the sentiment. "Thanks. What now?"

"Now, we go to dinner." He pulled a jacket from the back of the chair and slid his arms into the sleeves. "Did you enjoy your massage?"

I cast a look at him as he held the door for me. "You're watching me?"

"No, watching my credit account." He chuckled. "I'm glad you took advantage of the spa."

"I kind of wish I'd waited until after this meeting." I rubbed my arms.

He slung an arm around my shoulders and pulled me close to his warm body. "Maybe you'll have time for another before you leave."

I wasn't going to bet a single Lunatic on that.

We crept into the deserted tunnel and made our way to Dublin Dome. Nick stopped at one the nicer bars on a side street—a good step above anything I could afford.

We perched on tall stools beside an exterior bar, and Nick tapped the countertop to bring up the menu. When the robo-arm arrived, we took the glasses from the cup holders, and it whooshed away.

Nick clinked his glass against mine. "To a successful endeavor."

"That's nice and vague." I sipped my spritzer—a bit stronger than I was used to, so I'd better have only one.

He smiled and tapped his Ncuff. "Let me tell you about the program."

"Program?"

"I'm here for a board of directors' meeting, remember? I have to wrangle directors all day tomorrow. First meeting is at nine." He tapped his device again, and mine buzzed in response.

I opened the file and checked the schedule. "You have to attend all these meetings? Why am I here? I don't have to go to meetings, do I?"

He tapped the bottom entry. "You're here for the awards dinner. It's meant to be fun—but it probably won't be. Some of the directors bring their spouses. Oh, that reminds me—you can do the spouses' outing tomorrow, if you want."

"Spouses?" My cheeks went hot.

He smiled and winked. "That's why you're here—to give me some gravitas. Unmarried men aren't considered 'mature' in some circles on Lewei. My business is one of them. Anyway, they're touring some of the recreational areas in Port Royale and taking a walk on the lunar surface."

I glanced up. "I prefer to keep a thick layer of protection between me and the vacuum of space."

He slid off his stool and poked out an elbow for me to hold as we walked. "You haven't ever been outside?" He seemed genuinely interested in the answer.

"Fourth grade field trip. It's kind of boring out there. I mean, you can see the stars—and the planet—but you can see that on a vid."

"Fair enough. You don't have to go outside. But you should still go along for the rest. I've heard there might be shopping."

"Do I get an allowance?" I let go of his arm to hold out my hand.

"Didn't you find it? I stuck some Lunatics in your luggage."

"How did you manage that? The bag never left my sight, and yet you snuck that note—and apparently some cash—inside."

His eyes twinkled. "Trade secret." The grin faded. "Speaking of sneaking things—why didn't you tell me you had my cufflink?"

EPISODE 27: MAYBE I HAVE LOTS OF SECRET AGENT FRIENDS. YOU DON'T KNOW ME

I STOPPED in the middle of a tunnel. "Your cufflink? How did—what's special about it?"

"You have it, right? Did you happen to bring it with you?" He took my arm again and urged me into the throng in the Hub.

"You think I carry it around as a memento?" I tried to sound sarcastic, but my voice cracked on the last word. I looked away, my face burning.

"I hoped you'd realize it was important and bring it along." His deep, velvety voice slid along my nerves, smooth and soothing.

I coughed. "Actually, I do have it." I turned back to him, my voice strengthening with triumph. "I'm surprised you didn't find it when you were stuffing money and notes into my bag."

"Even I'm not good enough to search a bag while being watched." His lips twitched, and my insides flipped in response.

It really wasn't fair that he was so good looking. I flipped my long, dark hair over my shoulder, trying to be cocky and nonchalant. "If it was important, I'm sure you would have figured it out. Where are we going for dinner?" I stopped in surprise, looking around me. I hadn't been paying attention as we walked, but we'd left Dublin and moved on to Ibarra. "Why are we at Milo's Trading Post?"

Nick dropped our empty glasses into a recycler, grabbed my hand, and pulled me inside. "I figured we'd get picnic stuff and go to Tiergarten to eat."

"Isn't this supposed to be some all expenses paid, top drawer vacation?"

He let go of my hand to snag a basket. "For me, it's work, not a vacation. Tomorrow is the swanky part. Today, I'm an assistant on a tight paycheck trying to break even on a conference. I don't get a fat meal allowance and per diem payment like the board members—who don't really need the extra credits." He wrinkled his nose with a frown, sounding like every disgruntled mid-level employee ever. "How do you feel about a SuperCrunch Plate?" He pointed at a sign on the wall.

"I prefer the Honey-glazed Poultry Fry." We tapped the menu on the wall to order our takeout and picked it up at the other end of the store. "Any dessert? Mints, perhaps?"

He smirked and dropped a package of cookies on top of the healthier food. "Not tonight."

He carried our bag to the train, and we rode to Tiergarten Dome in comfortable silence. Like in Luna City, Tiergarten had a wide central plaza inside a series of connected domes with transparent tops. But instead of the Hills, Port Royale had sporting fields. Sports on Luna were played with heavier equipment to even the field for visiting Leweians and to improve muscle tone in locals. We settled on a bench beside a wide field where ten or twelve youngsters kicked a weighted soccer ball.

Nick tapped his Ncuff, and a low hum vibrated the base of my skull. He did something else, and the vibration faded.

"What was that?" I rubbed my neck.

"You felt it? Most people don't notice." He handed me a take-out box. "It's an audio disrupter. Anyone listening—electronically, not in person—will hear nothing."

"Why didn't you use that when we were at my apartment? Instead of the —" I waved my hands, and my face went nuclear.

"Where's the fun in that?" He smirked, then shrugged. "This will burn out any microphones in the area. If they planted one in your apartment, they'd be suspicious if it stopped working as soon as I walked in. Out here—if there's a mic, it's been here a while and listening to us is a coincidence."

I stared at him. "You think they bugged my apartment? Who's they? And why would they?"

He glanced at my fork, frozen halfway to my mouth. "Try to act natural. I don't know who they are. Could be mob. Could be Colonial or Gagarian. It's not a big deal—unless you make a habit of chatting up secret agents in your bedroom. What are they going to hear?"

My face flamed again. I lifted my chin, attempting dignity. "Maybe I have lots of secret agent friends. You don't know me."

He tapped my nose with his finger. "I know you better than you think. And don't let Betzy hear you say that about lots of agent friends. She's suspicious enough because of Marjatta."

I dropped my fork onto my meal. "Marjatta is my best friend and has never done anything remotely secret agent-ish."

"Her family is well-connected—which in Luna City means mob. And her mother, the admiral—well, the mob has completely infiltrated the lunar military."

"The mob?! Her family is mob? Then why did you want to meet her?" I'd always suspected the connection. As Nick pointed out, it was common knowledge that acquiring and holding wealth required mob connections. But to have it confirmed in such a matter-of-fact manner left me breathless. No one talked about the mob on Luna.

He took my fork and jabbed it into a piece of meat. "I need mob connections." When my mouth dropped open, he popped the food into it. "It's part of my job."

I snatched the fork out of his fingers and swallowed almost without chewing. "Marjatta is not mob! I won't have you using my friendship with her to do whatever it is you're—"

He put a warm finger against my lips. Startled by the touch, I fell silent. "I won't hurt Marjatta. It's her parents I need to meet, and your introduction will make that easier."

I cringed. Marjatta's parents had always been kind to me—in a kind of absent, barely noticing way. But I felt like I'd just sold them out to the enemy. "Wait. If you're LIA, why do you need me to make the connections? You said the mob is already in bed with the government."

He stared at the soccer players for a long moment as if lost in thought. Finally, he shrugged. "The LIA could have set up a meet. But doing it through you makes it look more real. That's why meeting you was a stroke of luck."

Was it? We still didn't know why Warenton set me up to meet Nick—or *if* he did. But maybe my relationship with Marjatta was the key. The idea made me squirm.

"Dessert?" Nick held a box of chocolate frosted cookies toward me. The rich scents of cocoa and vanilla wafted out of the open end.

I took one. "Thanks. Now tell me about the cufflink."

"It's a tracking device."

I gave him the stink eye. "If it was a tracking device, you'd know I brought it to Port Royale. Try again."

He chuckled and tapped the underside of my chin. "You're getting good at this stuff. It's another chip."

"Like the one that was in the mint tin?" When he nodded, I narrowed my eyes even more. "I don't believe it. You were so hot to get that chip, you crashed my party that night. I've had your cufflink for weeks. Try again."

"No, it really is a chip. I was supposed to pass it to my contact at the Varian, but then the whole beating up thing happened. I gave it to Warenton to pass on. Or so I thought. Apparently, you ended up with one of them. The chip only works if you have both parts."

I stared at the soccer players, absently stirring my fried veggies. "I find it hard to believe you lost track of it—and that you didn't come looking for it earlier."

"I was not operating at peak efficiency that night. Getting pistol whipped tends to mess with your cognitive capabilities. And I'm just the messenger—they don't always tell me what I'm passing or why."

"You still should have known you needed to give them both halves."

"Look, I screwed up—big time. But if you have it, I can—"

"I'm not buying it." I set the remains of my dinner on the bench and stood. "If you don't want to tell me the truth, that's fine, but don't insult me by coming up with half-baked lies."

"Katie—"

I flung up a hand to cut him off. "I don't want to hear anything but the truth. And right now, I'm going back to my hotel." I turned away, then spun back. "How's that going to work, anyway? They think you're a bell boy, not a guest."

He gathered up the remains of our dinner and shoved them into the bag. "No one notices the bell boys. Even the tall, handsome ones." He gave me a cheesy grin.

I mashed down my instinctive response and hardened my heart. "I don't understand any of this. You could have come to my room as yourself—you'll be seen with me tomorrow night, right? Why the bellboy thing? I'm starting to think this is all an elaborate prank."

He pushed the half-eaten package of cookies into a pocket and dropped the bag into the recycler, then reached out to take my hand. I pulled away. He gave me a reproving stare, and I slid my hand through his arm.

We walked along the edge of the soccer field and around the end before he spoke again. "Warenton is my mob connection. He's been an LIA informant for years, but my boss suspects he's up to something. I'm working with him...but watching him at the same time. That cufflink is a bug. I planted one on you and one on Warenton. We haven't heard anything useful from either of you." He gave me a wry grin.

I fought the urge to yell, "Ha!" He was finally telling me the truth—I could feel it—and I didn't want to interrupt.

"When I found out you knew Marjatta, I became more suspicious of Warenton's motives. Why did he try to put us together? Was it really a mistake—he thought you were Betzy? Or was there something else going on?"

After a few long seconds, I prompted, "Why did you ask me about the cufflink?"

He stopped walking and turned to look at me. "Because I like you. I trust you. Because no matter what Betzy says, I think—*I know*—you really are an innocent bystander, and I don't want to treat you like an enemy agent. But you need to know that being involved with me—even as cover—is risky. I'm working with the LIA and the mob. They play for keeps."

He picked up my hand from his arm, wrapping his fingers around mine. For the first time, they were cold, not warm. He squeezed my hand gently. "What do you say, Katie? Do you still want to help me?"

.

EPISODE 28: IT'S OH-DARK-UGLY, AND YOU'RE CALLING FROM A ROMANTIC GETAWAY

I STARED up into Nick's beautiful blue eyes. My heart pounded in my ears, and I had trouble pulling enough air into my lungs. I felt as though I'd reached a momentous decision point—as if Nick had offered me something valuable and fragile.

Which was ridiculous since all he'd asked was if I'd continue to help him.

But I knew a bit more about the stakes now. The lunar mob was dangerous. Deadly, even. And everyone knew they were in bed with the government, but no one talked about it. That kind of conversation could get you sent to the Xinjianestan re-education camp. No one ever completed the re-education process in Xinjianestan. Going there was a life sentence. And since it was located on a high-gravity planet, for someone raised on Luna, that sentence would likely be very short.

He squeezed my fingers again, pulling me a little closer. "Katie?"

My eyes snagged on his lips, full yet firm. I stepped closer, pulled in like a tractor beam. "Yes, Nick?"

"Will you help me?" He smiled hopefully, tentative and vulnerable.

My heart skittered around my chest like a mung-bird. "Of course."

"Great." He dropped my hand and strode along the baseline of the field.

Reality dumped over me like a bucket of ice water. Nick wanted to use me —an innocent civilian who would provide cover, nothing more. I needed to get my heart out of the equation and focus on the practical.

Nick turned around when he realized I was not keeping pace beside him. He frowned, then strode back to pull my hand through his arm again, dragging me with him. "We'll go back to the hotel. Tomorrow, you can sleep in and meet the other spouses in the lobby at ten. I'll catch up with you at dinner."

I stumbled along beside him, mentally cursing my decision to help. I was nothing to him, and I was letting him use me. I wouldn't go back on my word, but I'd armor my heart against his twinkling eyes and devastating smile. And once we got back to Luna City, cut all ties. I'd let myself get too wrapped up in the fiction, and now I was going to get hurt. Just like Marjatta said.

———

The next morning, I woke at daybreak. Artificial daybreak, of course, when the lights began to glow in the faux window beyond the curtains. I got up and dressed, careful to move quietly, so Nick wouldn't hear me in the adjoining room. Then I crept out of the hotel for a walk to clear my head.

I sucked in a breath of sanitized air and marched across the deserted central plaza of Paris Dome. A quick drop chute took me to the tunnels, and I hurried toward the trains. Two transfers later, the train dumped me in the Boston station, and I took a drop chute up to the plaza.

This wasn't my Boston, of course, but the newer-looking copy made me feel at home. I found an open coffee shop and ordered a cup. Then I found a table a safe distance from the other early morning customers and called Marjatta.

She picked up almost immediately. "Katie, are you all right?"

I squinted at her face on my Ncuff screen. "Of course. Why wouldn't I be?"

She covered a yawn with her hand. "Well, it's oh-dark-ugly, and you're calling from a romantic getaway."

"Oh, that. Yeah, it's not so romantic. He invited me because all of the bigwigs have wives, and he needed a date to fit in." I stirred my coffee, the recyclable spoon clicking against the plastek cup.

She pursed her lips. "Did you try the lingerie?"

"He's got a separate room. I'm not going to chase him down in my underwear. He made it very clear this is a completely platonic relationship."

"Well, in that case, you should go shopping. Charge everything to his room. You deserve some compensation for your trouble." She yawned again. "And tell him he can forget about our meeting next week. I'm no longer available to him."

"No!" The people in line whipped around to stare. "Sorry!" I waved them off and lowered my voice. "No, you should still meet with him. I didn't call you to—I'm not sure why I called."

"You called because I'm your best friend, and that's what you do when you're sad." Her face froze while she switched to another screen on her Ncuff, but her voice still came through. "I just rescheduled my day. I'll meet you in the Seasons lobby at 9:30. We'll go do something fun."

"I'm supposed to go on an excursion with the board members' spouses at ten."

"Perfect, I'll come with you. I haven't visited Port Royale since I was a kid. I hope they're going to the wax museum. I'll see you soon." She made a kissing noise at the screen, then the call ended.

That did not turn out the way I expected.

EPISODE 29: WE'LL PLUNDER THE MINI-BAR

I WASN'T sure what I expected when I called Marjatta. Some commiseration from a friend—and offers to cut Nick—socially, not physically. Which I got. But I didn't think she'd jump on the next train to hang out with me. Marjatta was a true friend.

By eight, I'd showered, dressed, and found a seat in the Seasons' coffee shop. My table stood by a window-like opening to the lobby, and an eye-water-ingly expensive bacon and egg sandwich sat beside another fragrant cup of coffee. I got a little thrill of satisfaction when I billed the meal to my room.

"Here you are!" Nick waved from the lobby, then disappeared into the restaurant, reappearing by my table. "I tried your room, but when you didn't answer I figured you were still asleep."

I shrugged and picked up my sandwich, sucking in the salty, greasy aroma of bacon. "I woke up, and I was hungry, so…" I left it hanging, daring him with my eyes to complain about my expensive meal choices.

"That smells fantastic." He waved down the waiter and ordered a matching sandwich and coffee—no orange juice. He was in full-on cover character mode. "Are you ready for a day of fun?"

"Yeah, Marjatta is joining me." I took a huge bite, and watched the emotions play across his face. I was expecting surprise and concern, but I only saw delight.

"That's marvelous. I'm sure the board members' spouses will love to meet her. You're both going on the tour, right?" The waiter delivered his coffee. Nick nodded thanks and turned back to me.

"I suggested we play hooky, but she wanted to do the excursion. She hasn't been to Port Royale in years."

"You were going to ditch the tour?" His brows drew together. "You were excited about going last night. What's wrong? Are you feeling sick?"

The concern in his eyes and voice cut me to the quick. I picked up my cup, reminding myself that he was a secret agent—a consummate actor. He would twist my emotions and use me if I let him. I sipped and set the coffee down. "Nothing's wrong. I figured the tour wasn't a big deal—I thought I was here primarily for the dinner."

He waggled his head side to side. "Yes and no. I mean, yeah, I need you at the dinner. But it will look odd if you don't attend the tour. And I thought you'd enjoy it—you've never been here before, right? I want you to have a good time." He slid his hand across the table and rested it on top of mine.

The waiter appeared with Nick's sandwich, giving me an excuse to pull my hand away. Every time he touched me, my brain went into neutral. I needed to keep my wits about me. "Don't worry, we're going. It will be fun if Marjatta is with me."

"I'd go if I could, but you know I'm working today." A hint of whine made his soothing voice grate.

I smirked and picked up my sandwich. "It's okay. We'll have more fun without you, anyway."

His eyes narrowed at me. "I'm sure you will. Don't do anything I wouldn't do."

I laughed. "I'm not sure I know you well enough to keep that promise."

He forced a dry chuckle and returned to his meal.

We'd just finished eating when Marjatta made her entrance. Even without her usual entourage, the woman knew how to draw every eye in the place. As she swept through the lobby, three hotel employees hurried forward to greet her. She waved them off and made a beeline toward me.

I jumped out of my chair to hug her through the little window, then gestured for her to join us. "Come on in—I can get you some coffee."

She held up an elegantly manicured hand and smirked. "I've had much too much caffeine this morning. Someone woke me at an unholy hour."

"Sorry."

"Darling, it's fine. I was bored with this weekend's schedule anyway. My father was entertaining some nabob from Lewei, and he wanted me to have lunch with them." She leaned forward and lowered her voice. "I think it was his idea of a blind date. I met him last night. No thanks." She gave a dramatic shudder. "He's ancient. And smelled of garlic." She turned her head to stare at Nick. "Citizen Beckett, how delightful to see you again." She didn't sound delighted.

Nick glanced at me, then stood, took Marjatta's hand, and bowed. "Lady Lipinski, the pleasure is all mine."

"No doubt. Katie, I need to freshen up. Can we go to your room?"

I tossed my napkin on the table. "Sure. See ya', Nick." Without waiting for a response, I hurried out of the restaurant and flung myself into Marjatta's arms.

"Whoa!" She gave me a swift hug, then set me back on my feet. "I have a reputation to uphold, even in Port Royale." Another hotel employee approached as we headed for the drop chutes, but she waved him away. "I'll check in later!"

"You can stay with me." We went up, and I opened the door to my room with a flourish. "The bed is big enough for ten of us."

"Where's he sleeping?" She dropped her bag on the luggage stand and roamed around the room, touching things here and there.

I pointed at an interior door. "Through there. It's locked on my side."

She nodded in satisfaction. "Excellent. I will stay here. And we'll plunder the mini-bar. Maybe call room service. I've heard the imported *terkfiske* is fabulous."

Marjatta changed clothes, then insisted I change as well. "You need to fit in with the group—I assure you none of them are wearing T-shirts and torn leggings." When she was satisfied with my appearance, we headed downstairs to meet the other spouses.

A group of ten men and women milled around the lobby. They all wore expensive clothing and ostentatious jewelry. Most of them were older—despite expert hair and facial modifications, their age was unmistakable. It was something about the way they moved—with the same assurance as Marjatta but slower and more weighty. Even the skinny woman with improbably blonde hair and eyelashes that looked like caterpillars.

Marjatta sailed into the center of the group, towing me along like a battered lifeboat. "Good morning, ladies and gentlemen. Citizen Beckett was kind enough to allow me to join you. I'm Marjatta Lipinski."

The spouses closed in around us, each of them eager to knock knuckles with Lady Lipinski. Apparently lunar celebrities were known on Lewei, too.

Once introductions were done—I didn't pay any attention, since everyone wore name tags—a handsome young man and woman approached the group. "Good morning," the woman said. "I'm Solena, and this is Hercule. We'll be your guides today. Please, follow us." The pair executed a synchronized turn and led the group toward the drop chutes.

On the lower floor, we climbed into a private train car owned by the hotel and whooshed away. Marjatta and I sat across a small table from Frieda and Pierce. Frieda explained her husband was chair of the board of directors, and Pierce's wife was the vice chair.

Throughout the day, they clung to us—or rather, to Marjatta—like burrs. At each stop, Frieda and Pierce closed in on either side of Marjatta, taking her arm, sending Solena and Hercule running for drinks, chairs, snacks, whatever they thought Marjatta might want. I trailed along behind with the rest of the spouses, through the wax museum, the Port Royale power station, the high-end stores in Beijing, and the local Varian Center—which looked exactly like the one in Luna City. By the end of the day, I was exhausted, but Marjatta, Frieda, and Pierce had become the best of friends.

About four o'clock, we arrived in the Tiergarten airlock. Solena stood in front of the wide window that allowed visitors to view the surface of the moon and spread her arms. Her white Seasons Hotel uniform glowed against the gray-red landscape. "This is our last stop, but we have time for a quick excursion. Who wants to experience the surface of Luna?"

"Will we have to walk?" Frieda put a hand to her ample bosom. "This day has been exhausting."

"The light gravity is completely misleading, isn't it?" Pierce gushed. "I thought it would be so relaxing but walking still requires all the same muscles." He giggled. "I guess I need to get into better shape before my next visit."

"We'll suit up and go out in a rover." Solena gestured, and the window behind her darkened to show a video. A lumpy looking vehicle rolled through wide doors and across the lunar surface. Vacuum-suited individuals waved through the windows. Then a map appeared, showing the vehicle's relative location to the dome. "We'll travel about three kilometers, until you can no longer see the dome, so you feel the isolation." She widened her eyes. "It's not for the faint of heart! Those who wish may exit the vehicle to experience the surface for about twenty minutes." On screen, a family leapt across the landscape, with a soundtrack of laughter and excited but unintelligible conversation.

"Our suits are limited to only forty minutes of air, so we'll get back in the vehicle and return to the airlock. Who wants to join in the fun?" She beamed at the small crowd. After a brief pause, Pierce's hand shot into the air, and everyone else followed suit.

"Peer pressure." I glanced at Marjatta. "Are you going out?"

She shuddered delicately. "And end up with a holey suit and a low air tank? No thank you." Our eyes met. Hers held none of the humor I expected. Then she smiled and laughed unconvincingly.

I forced a chuckle. "Have you ticked off the mob?"

"Not recently." She gave her head a little shake, as if to throw off her tension. "It's an old joke in the family."

Now that I knew Marjatta's family had mob connections, it wasn't so funny.

On her way to the suit room, Frieda stopped beside us. "Lady Lipinski, aren't you coming?"

Marjatta heaved a dramatic sigh. "Been there, done that. We'll be waiting for you here." She subsided onto a bench facing the panoramic windows. I dropped to the seat beside her.

"We can't have you sitting here alone! Pierce, maybe you should stay." Frieda grabbed the man's arm as he trundled past.

I opened my mouth to object, but Marjatta patted my arm. "I'm not alone. I have my dear friend Katie to keep me company. Do go on. Enjoy." She turned away, clearly indicating the conversation was finished.

Frieda glared at me over Marjatta's shoulder, then stomped away with Pierce on her heels. Solena and Hercule rounded up the others, and they disappeared into the suit room.

When the room finally emptied, I leaned against the wall and closed my eyes. "That was… a lot. I'm glad they're gone for a while. So much neediness."

"Try being me." Marjatta's defeated voice touched a chord in my soul.

My eyes popped open. "Are you okay?"

She shrugged. "I'm fine. This life puts a lot of expectations on me. That's why I was so happy to get your call—it gave me an excuse to get out of some things."

"And I dumped you back into it." I waved at the door through which our companions had disappeared.

She waved a negligent hand. "Not to worry. I can handle brown-nosers and wannabees. If I have to. But what do you say we jump ship? I could use a drink."

"Works for me." I tapped my Ncuff and sent a quick message to Solena. "Let's get out of here."

EPISODE 30: I'M ALWAYS PREPARED TO GO INCOGNITO

WE HOPPED A TRAIN TO LAD—LOS Angeles Dome. In Luna City, Lad was one of the lower-income domes—mostly residential, with a few lower-cost restaurants. A convenient place to grab a quiet drink without attracting too much attention. As we rode, Marjatta removed her jewelry and tucked it into the hidden side pockets of her close-fitting pants. She pulled the pins from her hair and swept it up into a ponytail, pulling wispy bangs around her face. Then she folded her flowing, robe-like jacket inside out, and it became a non-descript backpack.

I stared—this woman still looked like my friend, but different. I hadn't seen her so dressed down since school. "You just went from socialite to salaryman in about five minutes."

A quick grin zipped across her face and disappeared. "I'm always prepared to go incognito."

We stepped off the train. The Lad station was noisy—in one corner, a group of men argued about something. The smell of onions and fuel washed over us, and my stomach rolled. I swallowed hard, thankful I hadn't eaten recently.

A gang of children surrounded us, begging for change. Marjatta pulled some coins from one of her many pockets and tossed them to the kids. The money disappeared like water into the lunar sand, and the kids scattered.

Behind us, a man spoke. "You must know magic—whenever I give anyone money, a dozen more appear to get their share."

Marjatta turned and showed her teeth in a "don't mess with me" grin. "They can sense your intentions. If you project 'this is it, get it now or not at all,' they can feel it."

"Your terrifying smile doesn't hurt," I muttered.

We took the drop chute to the main level. This dome bore little resemblance to the Lad in Luna City. Sure, the basic structure was identical—buildings grouped around a central plaza with "streets" extending outward. But graffiti covered many of the dirty walls, and some of the windows were blocked with rigid plastek sheets, which were also tagged in strangely somber colors. Clusters of mean-looking locals loitered in dark doorways. Even the overhead lights that mimicked the sun seemed dimmer.

I stepped closer to Marjatta. "Are you sure this is a good place to get a drink? It looks a little dodgy."

"A little?" She swaggered forward a few steps but lowered her voice. "Stay close but look mean."

I took a couple of running steps to catch up. "I'm barely a meter and a half tall. How am I supposed to look mean?"

"You're all buff from working out—pretend you're one of those weightlifters from Lewei who likes to show off how much they can lift on Luna."

I smothered a nervous laugh. Those guys were so ridiculous—everyone knew gravity was lighter here. But they insisted on loading up their barbells with the heaviest plates, just to show how strong they were. I pulled my shoulders back, lifted my chin, and strutted after Marjatta. "Can't we just leave?"

"If we turn around, we look scared. We're here for a reason, and we aren't going to let these punks stop us." She strutted toward the only bar that appeared to be open. As she approached, a couple of tall, skinny men broke away from their gang and moved to intercept us.

"Wha' choo doin' here, princess?" The shorter one stepped in front of Marjatta.

She looked him up and down, raised an eyebrow, then pushed past him, ramming her shoulder against his arm to shove him out of the way. "None of your business, punk."

"Punk?" The skinny guy smirked at his friend and clapped a hand to his chest. "She called me a punk, Romeo. I'm deeply wounded."

Romeo shook his head slowly as the rest of the crew moved closer. "That is just not right, Percival." He moved in front of Marjatta, blocking her again. "You're not bein' very nice to my boy Percy."

"Your *boy* shouldn't mess with women he doesn't know." Marjatta pushed past Romeo. I scuttled along behind her, trying to look formidable.

Romeo grabbed my arm. "Maybe your little friend will talk to us."

"Let go of me!" My demand came out a terrified plea.

Marjatta stopped, not turning. "Let go of my friend, if you value your fingers."

The two men laughed. "Wha' choo gonna do, Prin—"

Before he could finish, Marjatta whipped around. In a lightning-fast move, she ripped his hand from my arm and twisted.

Romeo shrieked in pain, whirling around until Marjatta held his hand behind his back. "She's breaking my arm!" His band of followers closed in around us.

Marjatta shifted her grip, and Romeo cried out again. She held his hand in a seemingly negligent fashion, but the man quivered and staggered. Marjatta gave him another tweak and raised one eyebrow at Percival. "One step closer, and I start snapping bones."

"Clear off!" Romeo gasped.

The men exchanged wary glances, then faded away. Percival loitered near the closest doorway, clearly reluctant to leave his comrade.

Marjatta loosened her grip but didn't let go. "My friend and I are going to get a drink. Perhaps you can recommend somewhere?"

"The Bird and Bat is good." Percival jerked a thumb over his shoulder.

Marjatta released Romeo's hand. "Would you care to join us?"

Why would she invite them to join us? I gulped but kept my mouth shut.

Romeo glanced at Percival, and the two seemed to hold a silent conversation. Then Romeo gave a single jerky nod. Marjatta strode forward, and the two men dropped in on either side, giving her plenty of space. When they reached the door, Romeo opened it and held it wide for Marjatta.

She turned. "Katie, aren't you coming?"

I jerked out of my stupor and hurried across the rough plaza, trying to swagger and move quickly at the same time. Note to self: doing both is impossible.

Like the plaza, the bar was dark and dingy. A man with unkempt white hair growing in a fringe around the sides of his head stood behind the counter polishing a glass. A man and a woman sat at opposite ends of the bar, ignoring everyone as they nursed their drinks. Battered chairs stood near a scattering of equally decrepit tables, and the sour air reeked of spilled beer and rancid peanuts.

It looked like the set for a violent vid game.

Marjatta took a seat against a wall and gestured for us to join her. I grabbed the sturdiest looking chair and sat, unsure it would support even my relatively small mass. The chair groaned, but it held. Percival and Romeo pulled two more chairs to the table but kept their distance from Marjatta.

When she raised her hand, the bartender scurried around the end of the bar to Marjatta. "Vodka. An unopened bottle and four glasses. Make sure they're clean." She slid a paper Lunatic to the man in a move I almost missed. The man rubbed his fingers over the bill without looking, then nodded and disappeared through a back door.

I leaned closer to Marjatta and dropped my voice. "I don't really drink vodka."

She gave me the stink eye. I shrank back into my seat.

Marjatta was my best friend, but sometimes, I barely recognized her. When we were at fancy functions, like the party at her parents' house or the Varian Center, she acted the flighty socialite. Other times, like the coffee meeting with Nick, she embodied the slick CEO. In that dingy bar, she projected "terrifying thug," and I could one hundred percent believe Nick's suggestion that she was part of the mob. Who was the real Marjatta?

The only thing I knew for sure was she was my best friend. I hoped my trust was not misplaced.

We waited in silence. Percival and Romeo fidgeted while Marjatta sat like a stone statue on her rickety chair. Finally, the bartender returned with a tray. He deposited the bottle on the table, then poured some water from a pitcher into a glass. He swirled it around and drank from it. Then he poured water into four more glasses, swirled them, and dumped them into the first glass and drank the lot. He set the newly rinsed glasses on the table, taking his glass away on the tray.

I'd seen that exact ritual on a vid—the bartender proving the glasses weren't poisoned. Who knew it was a real thing?

Obviously, my three companions did.

Marjatta unsealed the bottle and poured a little into one glass. She swirled it around and dumped the remains on the floor, then poured a generous serving of the vodka into the glass and handed me the bottle. I copied her actions, adding a smaller amount to my glass, and passed the bottle on. The men didn't bother rinsing their glasses—maybe they felt confident the bartender wouldn't poison them.

Marjatta raised her glass. "To new associates."

The three of us toasted in return, murmuring the same words. The men tossed their vodka back and refilled their glasses. Marjatta sipped hers. I put the glass to my lips, then set it on the table, untasted. The stuff smelled like solvent.

Romeo reached inside his loose jacket. Beside me, Marjatta froze. The man caught her eye and held his coat away from his body, revealing a stunner strapped to his hip. Why hadn't he used that when Marjatta twisted his arm? He reached into an inner pocket of the coat and extracted a small card which he dropped on the center of the table. "My treat."

It was a standard pre-paid bancard, the kind that allowed the user to make purchases without his Ncuff. Theoretically, they prevented the merchant from collecting the buyer's personal data, since they weren't connected directly to a bank account. But the government could trace who had purchased them and where the money was loaded. The only way to be truly anonymous was to buy one with cash. And that had its own perils.

Why was he offering to pay? Had he not seen Marjatta pass the cash to the bartender?

Marjatta nodded regally. "My thanks."

Romeo poured shots into his glass and Percival's, then offered the bottle to Marjatta. She lifted her glass and sipped, then shook her head. They didn't even look at me.

The men downed their shots and set their glasses on the table. Romeo screwed the lid back onto the bottle, and it disappeared into this voluminous coat. They stood and bowed. "It was a pleasure doing business with you," Percival muttered. He didn't sound pleased.

When Marjatta nodded again, they disappeared through the door without a backward glance.

I twisted around in my chair. "What the heck just happened?"

Marjatta set her half-full glass on the table and stood. The bancard disappeared into her pocket as she dropped a few more Lunatics on the table. "We had a drink with new friends. Let's go."

EPISODE 31: ONE MISTAKE CAN DERAIL YOUR ENTIRE CAREER

WE TOOK the drop chute to the train level.

"What's the deal with the bancard?" I whispered.

Marjatta gave me a narrow-eyed look. "It's not just a bancard." She didn't explain any further, but I could guess: it was a data chip.

When we stepped out of the drop chute, we stood in one of those dark tunnels like the ones below the Varian Center.

Marjatta froze. "Katie, get back into the chute." She pushed me behind her, pulling a stunner from one of her hidden pockets.

"Where were you hiding that?" I stumbled into the drop chute, but it didn't activate.

"Quiet." She backed closer, her head swiveling from side to side as she peered into the dim passage.

"It's not working." I tapped my Ncuff and opened the drop chute app, but it wouldn't connect. "The chute is broken."

"It's not broken." A man stepped out of the dark, pointing a weapon at Marjatta. He wore a black uniform with three red stripes on the sleeve and the symbol of the Lunar Jingcha—the local police force—on the chest. "You're both under arrest for passing stolen information. Drop your weapon."

Marjatta sighed and put the stunner on the floor near her feet. She straightened and pushed the weapon with her foot, sliding it over the smooth plascrete to the jingcha. "This is a mistake I hope won't derail your entire career."

The jingcha's face blanched, but he stood his ground. "Hands on your head. Turn around slowly."

I snapped my hands to my head as Marjatta turned. Her eyes met mine, then flicked to the floor. I followed her gaze. The bancard Romeo left on the table now lay on the floor of the drop chute.

"You, too, girl! Turn around!"

I shuffled forward a half step as I turned, setting the ball of my foot over the card. Rough hands yanked my arms down one at a time, tightening something around each wrist. Then they pulled me around to face the opening. I put all my weight on my right foot as they pivoted me, hoping I could keep the card hidden.

But then what? Marjatta clearly didn't want them to find that card. As soon as they pushed me out of the chute, it would become visible. Where—*how* could I hide it?

The jingcha on my right jerked me toward the door. I dragged my feet, scraping the card forward—I hoped.

"Do you want to add resisting arrest to your charges?" the jingcha snarled.

"I'm not resisting!" I shoved my foot forward again, aiming for the gap between the drop chute floor and the doorway. I let my left leg buckle a little and shuffled to the right as if trying to regain my balance. "You shoved me!"

As the man hauled me through the opening, I dragged both feet again, then stumbled forward, taking a second to peek at the floor behind me.

Nothing.

Either I'd succeeded in dropping the card through the gap, or it was stuck to my shoe. The thin sole didn't feel any different under my foot. I'd have to hope for the best.

The jingcha stomped down the hallway, pulling me roughly with him. He managed to ram me into the wall more than once as we walked, his hand squeezing my arm in a vice.

We took a different drop chute up a few levels, stepping out into a dingy lobby. Percival and Romeo sat on a bench by the wall, their hands and legs fastened to metal rings with plastek ties. Neither of them acknowledged us in any way as the jingcha paraded us through another door.

We walked along another gloomy corridor, then the man ahead of me opened a door on the right. My minder shoved me through and slammed the door shut behind me.

I stood in the middle of a tiny cell. The bench along one wall held a thin blanket and no mattress. A metal toilet squatted in the corner. A very obvious camera hung above, its red light glaring like a demonic eye.

I wrapped the blanket around my body and sat on the cold bench. Although lunar cities were usually quite warm, thanks to the heat generated by the oxygen plants, this room was frigid. The cold seeped into my muscles and bones, draining me.

After a while, I got up and jogged in place. The activity warmed me and kept my mind from wandering into the dark stories I'd heard about jingcha captives my whole life. The Lunar Jingcha had a less ominous reputation than the Leweian Guard, but not by much. Every citizen knew crossing the law was a bad idea.

Muscles warmed by the exertion, I switched to strength exercises. The equipment in the gym offered a more complete workout, but old-fashioned push-ups and sit-ups were better than nothing. I focused on counting reps and my breathing.

Finally, I collapsed on the bench, wrapping the blanket around myself again. Although I was sweaty and hot, the cold air bit through my damp clothing like icy fingers.

I checked my Ncuff. Strange that they hadn't taken the device. But it refused to connect to the NexUs. My apps were frozen, and my on-device data was inaccessible. Somehow, they'd nullified the device without touching it. Only the time showed—I'd been locked up for about two hours.

I lay down on the bench, but the cold kept me awake. My mind trotted out every jingcha horror story I'd ever heard: people taken away and never heard from again, prisoners tortured or forgotten, and of course, deportation to Xinjianestan prison camp. In fact, I couldn't remember a single story where an innocent victim had been questioned and released.

Which brought up another question: was I really innocent? Nick claimed to work for the Lewei Intelligence Agency. Because Luna was a province of Lewei, working for the LIA should make him a good guy, right?

But according to Betzy, Marjatta's family was mob, or had mob affiliations. And the mob was in bed with the lunar government. Which should be the same side as the LIA.

Except the lunar government constantly lectured the citizenry about ending corruption. According to the news reports, mob bosses were sent off to Xinjianestan all the time.

Which side did that put me on?

———

My door clanged open, and a man stood in the opening, wearing a Leweian Guard uniform with lots of gold stars on the collar. A scarce bristle of hair accentuated the skull-like shape of his face. His narrow shoulders and tall, angular physique added to the skeletal appearance. He smiled, showing tiny teeth like a baby. Creepy. "Let's have a chat."

I jumped to my feet. I wasn't an expert on Leweian Guard rank, but this guy had more bling than anyone I'd ever seen, even Marjatta's mother the admiral.

He strode into the room and snapped his fingers. Two jingcha, each bearing one lowly stripe, dragged a large, upholstered chair to the center of the room, then retreated to either side of the door. The officer sat and opened a compartment on the arm of the chair. He fiddled with something inside and then relaxed into the thick cushion with a sigh. "These heated seats are truly an ingenious invention, aren't they?"

I perched on the edge of the bench. "I wouldn't know."

His dark eyes narrowed.

"Sir," I added.

He smiled. The death's-head grin chilled me more than the cold bench. "Why are you here, Citizen?" The voice was light and gentle, almost nurturing.

"I was hoping you could tell me that." I wrapped the blanket more tightly around my body, trying to stop my shivering. "I was having a drink with my friend, and then the jingcha dragged us in here."

"Ah, yes, your friend." His expression darkened. "She has been most unhelpful in my investigation."

I was cold, hungry, and terrified. I just wanted out, and this man was the first person to speak to me in hours. He clearly held the keys to my predicament, and if I just cooperated, like a good citizen, I could go home. But a cold, analytical section of my mind had switched on, and I noticed things I should have been too scared to see.

My visitor—I decided to call him the general—hadn't mentioned my name. Did he know it? Scraping my name from my Ncuff should have been easy—and standard procedure. He also hadn't mentioned Marjatta's name.

His uniform didn't fit well. Either he'd lost a lot of weight recently, or this wasn't his clothing. I focused on his bling. He had both medals and ribbons pinned to his chest—surely that wasn't normal? In fact, the one on the second row looked like the "real military medal" we sold at LCL. I squinted. Were those crossed cannons on the gold circle?

The general slapped his hand on the chair arm, and I jumped. "Are you listening to me?" His voice crackled with fury, but his eyes looked worried. Did he think I wasn't falling for his act?

I faked a smothered sob. "Sorry. It's just so cold, and I'm…" I let my voice trail off.

He leaned forward, elbows on his knees, and smiled the creepy smile again. "I want to help you, young lady, but you need to help me first."

Close up, I could see that his eyebrows had been darkened—maybe to make him more threatening? Or to hide his identity.

"What do you want?" I whispered.

"Information."

EPISODE 32: BETZY SMITH IS AN UNUSUAL NAME

I HUNCHED my shoulders and clutched my blanket tightly around my body. The cold made my teeth chatter—I hoped it made me look vulnerable and scared. Could I get him to offer some concessions? "I want to help, sir, but I'm so cold."

The general snapped his fingers. "Get our guest a thicker blanket. And something warm to drink."

The skinnier guard saluted and left the room.

The general sat back in his chair and steepled his fingers. "What is your name?"

What should I say? Was he gauging my truthfulness, or did he really not know? What would Marjatta want me to answer? I might have had doubts about her affiliation with the mob, but she had never given me reason to question our friendship. I'd trust she had my best interests at heart until she proved otherwise. And that meant keeping her name secret.

Or at least that seemed like the best plan. But what name should I give? "Betzy. Betzy Smith."

"That's an unusual name."

The guard returned with the blanket and a steaming mug. He started toward me, but the general held up a hand. "What is your friend's name?"

"My friend?" I did my best blank stare. *Keep it simple, Katie.* "Oh, you mean Marge? She's not really my friend. I met her on the tour. If I'd known she was going to get me into trouble, I wouldn't have agreed to get a drink with her."

"What tour?"

"I'm here with my boyfriend, Nick. He helped set up some meeting for the bigwigs at his company. They sent the spouses—and me—on a tour of the city. That's where I met Marge." I looked hopefully at the guard holding the blanket.

The general nodded, and the flunky handed me the blanket. While I wrapped it around myself, the general continued his questions. "What is Marge's last name?"

I looked up in feigned surprise and froze. "I don't know. Like I said, we just met."

He held up a hand, stopping the guard from passing the mug to me. "But surely you know her surname. Or her husband's name."

I bit my lip. "Why would I know that? I've never met him."

"You said he's an important member of your boyfriend's company. What's his name?"

I whimpered and cowered in my blanket. "I really don't know. I've only been with Nick a few weeks. We don't talk about his work."

The general let out a heavy sigh and motioned to the guard. The man handed me the mug. I wrapped my frozen hands around the thick plastek, cradling the warmth close to my chest before sipping the bitter, black coffee.

The general heaved himself out of the armchair and motioned to his goons. "Turn the chiller off. She doesn't know anything."

"Thank you, sir." I smiled tremulously. "Can I have the heated chair?"

"No." He snapped his fingers and marched out of the room. The goons dragged the chair out behind him.

I sipped the coffee, then pulled the blanket up over my head to keep the heat in. And to hide my smile.

And the little piece of paper I peeled from the bottom of the mug. Under the cover of the blanket, I smoothed it out.

I'll get you out soon.

N.

I curled up inside my new, warm cocoon and went to sleep.

––––––

The clink of the door lock woke me. I blinked into the darkness, trying to get my bearings. The door shut, leaving me in darkness again. Even the camera light was gone. A light flared, illuminating my little cell.

"Katie, where are you?"

"Nick!" I rolled out from under the bench, bringing my blankets with me.

He reached a hand to pull me up and wrapped both arms around me. "Are you okay? Did they hurt you?" A tremor rattled his voice.

"I'm fine. The general—he isn't really a Leweian Guard." I snaked my arms around him, pressing my face to his chest, my distrust of his motives temporarily forgotten.

He went still. "How do you know?"

I explained about the phony medal.

Nick relaxed a fraction and chuckled. "I guess they should source their wardrobe more carefully."

"You don't sound surprised." I released him and stepped back, squinting in the light of his Ncuff. "You knew they were fake. What's going on?"

"Let's get out of here. We can talk later."

My eyes narrowed, and I plopped down on the bench. "No, we can talk now. What's going on?"

"Katie, we have to escape. Before they notice I've taken their camera offline."

I crossed my arms. "Yeah, why haven't they noticed that?"

"Because they're short-staffed? How would I know?" He shoved a hand through his hair and gritted his teeth. "I'm not familiar with their operating procedures, but I think we should get out while we have the chance!"

"What about Marjatta?"

"What about her? She's in the next cell. We'll grab her and go."

"I'm not sure I'm buying this whole thing."

"What are you talking about, Katie?" His voice ratcheted up a few notches.

"You've made it very clear you're using me to get to Marjatta. How do I know you didn't set this fake abduction up so you can be the hero and gain her trust?"

"Do you really think I'd be stupid enough to use a novelty from your company on a costume?" His voice sounded choked as he checked the time. "You weren't at dinner, you didn't answer when I called your room or your Ncuff, so I came looking for you."

"How did you find me? I don't have that cufflink on me."

He grabbed my arm and pulled me up from the bench. "Katie, we need to go. Now."

I dropped my blankets—the cell was a normal temperature now. "Fine. But I'm having trouble believing this is real."

The door lock clicked again, and we spun toward the sound.

A man stood in the doorway. "It's very real, Katie Li."

"Warenton!" Nick's voice was gruff with disbelief. "What are you doing here?"

"Welcome to the party, my boy." Warenton strolled into the room. Behind him, two men lurked in the hallway—the two guards who'd come with the general earlier. "I was hoping you'd arrive."

"What—"

Warenton pointed at the bench. "You might want to sit down while I monologue like a video villain."

I sank to the bench. "Why would you do that?"

"Good point." Warenton stepped back into the hallway. "You don't need to know what I'm doing and why." He glanced at the guards. "Kill them and dispose of the bodies."

"Wait!" Nick cried, but Warenton walked away.

The two guards moved forward, drawing their blasters. "Get up," one of them said.

I crossed my arms over my chest. "Maybe we won't."

"Katie, don't antagonize them."

"What difference does it make? They're going to kill us whether we cooperate or not. I'm not going out with a whimper." I glared at the guard closest to me, then reached forward and ripped the medal off his chest. It matched the one the general wore.

"Hey!"

"You probably shouldn't buy your military bling from a novelty company."

The guy ground his teeth. "Get up and get moving."

"Not going to happen. If you want to kill me, you'll have to do it here and drag my cold, dead body to wherever you want to go." I never realized I had a split personality before now. But the terrified part of my mind had retreated into a mental castle and pulled up the drawbridge, leaving the crazy person in charge.

"I don't want to drag a body—it looks suspicious." My guard—I decided to call him Scrawny—waved his blaster at me.

"Just pick her up and carry her." The rounder guard—now dubbed Rolly—waved his weapon at Nick.

Scrawny put his weapon into his holster and moved toward me. I leaped up from the bench and darted past Nick and Rolly.

"Hey, stop running away!"

"Or what? You'll kill me? You need to learn to set your threats at a lower level. Starting with the most devastating leaves you nowhere to escalate." I circled behind the other two men.

"Stop." Rolly jerked his weapon at Nick. "Move, or I'll shoot your friend."

Nick took a half-step toward the door, but Rolly jerked the weapon again. "Her—I want her to move, not you."

"Fine." I flung up both hands in surrender, then bolted out the door.

EPISODE 33: HE TOLD HIS GOONS TO KILL US

I RACED DOWN THE HALL, ignoring the yells coming from behind me. A blaster fired, and my heart seemed to stop beating, but I kept running. Nick would have to take care of himself. I needed to escape and find a weapon. And an ally. I skidded around a corner and slammed into someone.

"Katie, you got out—nice job!"

I took a step back, pressing my hand to my chest. "Marjatta? Wha—how did you get out?"

"I have my ways. Have you seen Warenton?"

I gaped at her. How did she know Warenton? "He just told his goons to kill us."

"Us?" As the word left her mouth, her eyes slid over my shoulder and snagged on something.

I spun around to see Rolly and Scrawny on either side of Nick, dragging him down the corridor.

"Ah, Nick. Thanks for coming. Gentlemen, you can release him."

All three men stopped and stared at Marjatta.

"You want us to let him go?" Rolly's blaster drooped.

Nick shook off Scrawny's hand and strutted toward us. "Thank you for the assistance, my lady."

"Quiet." Marjatta snapped out the word without sparing a glance for Nick. "You two, find Mr. Warenton and bring him to me."

The men spun on their heels and disappeared around the corner. I scuffled back a couple of steps. Why were these goons following Marjatta's directions?

Marjatta turned and strode the other way. "Come with me."

"Wha—"

She cut Nick off. "We'll talk later." A twinge of satisfaction warmed my chest. It was only fair that Nick get the same answer he'd given me. "We need to go."

Marjatta led us through a door and up some stairs, then down another corridor. She unlocked each door with her Ncuff. "Make sure those are closed behind us."

A few minutes later, we reached a familiar tunnel. "This leads back to Paris. I recommend you return to your hotel and finish your trip." Marjatta glanced at the closed door behind Nick. "And don't come back here."

"You're coming with us, aren't you?" I grabbed Marjatta's arm.

She pulled away from my hand. "I need to retrieve that card you hid—well done, Katie. And I need to take care of Warenton."

"What do you mean, by 'take care of' him?" My voice trembled.

"Don't ask the question if you don't want to know the answer." Marjatta pulled me in for a quick hug. She put her lips against my ear, speaking softly. "Be careful with Nick. I don't trust him one hundred percent." She released me, opened the door behind her, and disappeared down the corridor.

I dragged my eyes from the closed door and looked at Nick. "I don't even know what to ask. But when I figure it out, you'd better tell me the truth." I turned away, striding toward Paris Dome.

"Katie, wait." Nick dropped into step beside me. "I'll explain everything. I promise—no lies."

I held up a hand. "Later. I'm too tired to even think about it." I stumbled, and he took my arm. When we reached Paris Dome, the central plaza was quiet—it was too late even for the partiers that made Port Royale famous. We trudged into the hotel and took the drop chute to our floor.

I waved my Ncuff at my door before remembering it had been wiped. But the door popped open. When I tapped the device, it lit up with my usual start screen. Nick opened his mouth, but I waved him off. "Later." I wobbled across the room, dimly noticing the door shut behind me, and fell onto the bed, face first.

———

My door chimed, and I peeled my eyes open. Faux sunlight streamed into the room. I sat up and glanced at the mirror across from the bed. My hair stood at all angles, my makeup was smeared, and my clothing was wrinkled. About par for the night.

"Room service," a familiar voice called.

I padded across the room and peered at the access screen. A tall, blond man with the smile of a Norse god stood behind a cart covered with a white cloth.

He looked at the camera, and his blue eyes twinkled. My heart did a little jump, then settled down to double-time.

I opened the door, trying to keep my face blank. "Thank you. Bring it inside." As I stepped back, he pushed the cart into the room. Bacon, cinnamon, and butter beckoned me closer, so I followed him across the room, letting the door shut behind me. He pulled the white cloth off and flipped it onto the small table by the faux window. Then he whisked the curtains open to show off the phony view—it looked like a famous scene from Lewei City. The city gleamed in the sunlight, autos streaking by on slender, shimmering ribbons wrapped around the buildings, and the sea glittered under the sun in the distance. He set two places and poured coffee and juice. "Have a seat."

I stood beside my chair, fiddling with a knife. "Don't you have to return the cart? Won't they be suspicious if you stay to eat with me?"

He shrugged and settled into the other chair. "No one is watching. And if they are, I don't care. I'm having breakfast—brunch really—with my girlfriend."

"Brunch?!" In a panic, I smacked my Ncuff. "It's after eleven! I've missed my gym session!"

His brows drew down, and his lips twitched. "You scheduled a workout for Sunday morning?"

"I work out *every* morning." I tapped my Ncuff and pulled up the health center calendar. "They don't have room for me before my train back to Luna City!"

"The world won't end if you don't exercise today."

I swiped through a couple of screens and scheduled a session at my home gym for that evening. "You don't understand. Working out is my ticket to travel. We Lunites have to keep fit if we're going to survive on regular planets."

He stood and nudged me into my chair, pulling it close to the table. "Missing one session won't end your dream. Besides, I might be able to help you with that."

"What do you mean?"

He handed me a serving spoon. "Eat and I'll tell you."

We ate in silence for a while, enjoying the steamed buns, rice porridge, and scallion eggs. I finished my plate and leaned back in my chair. "I want to know what happened last night."

He held up a hand, stopping me, then swiped his Ncuff. A low hum vibrated the base of my neck—the jammer.

"Aren't you worried about someone noticing the mics in this room went out?"

He smirked. "I spent the morning taking out mics on random floors. They won't even blink."

I took a deep breath, not completely sure I wanted to know everything, now that I had the chance to ask. "Why did those people listen to Marjatta? Why did Warenton want to kill us? And how did you find me?"

He sipped his juice, made a face, and put it back on the table. "I can't believe you've gotten me to like coffee." He poured some cream and spooned a lot of sugar into a mug, then filled it with hot coffee.

"That's not coffee, that's candy."

"Still, I've drunk so much in the last few weeks, I kind of like it." He sipped the brew, then added a little more cream. "I told you Marjatta is connected to the mob." He fiddled with his spoon, not meeting my eyes. "I found you because I lied."

I waited for my heart to sink, but it didn't bother. "What else is new?"

"Ouch. But I deserved that. My life is lying." He tapped the spoon against the table, then dropped it. "You know I'm an agent. I work for the Leweian Intelligence Agency."

I nodded, making a "go on" motion.

"What you don't know is I'm a double agent. I work for the Leweian Freedom Federation."

This time, my heart dropped like a rock, and my stomach went queasy. "They're a terrorist group!"

"Resistance organization. There have been zero terrorist attacks connected to the LFF. They're trying to reform the Leweian political structure to allow more freedom. Did you know in other systems, citizens don't have to join a brainwashing cult as children to receive permission to leave their home planet? They don't fear being picked up by jingcha agents and dumped into a 're-education camp' if they express discontent. Or talk about the government being in bed with the mob. They don't even have a mob."

I swallowed. The terror inspired by the threat of Xinjianestan had left me cold and shaking the night before. Was it possible other systems didn't have such a menace? But still, did I want to be a freedom fighter?

A little voice in the back of my head cheered, as if this was what she'd been waiting for all my life.

I shook my head trying to dislodge her. "What does that have to do with last night?"

"Marjatta is mob. Warenton is mob. He thought you were trying to move in on something he's got going here in Port Royale—that's why he had you two 'arrested' by his fake Leweian guards. But he didn't realize how far up the food chain Marjatta is. He thought he was disposing of a couple of minor inconveniences. I think he's really after me. For some reason, he blames me for his son's death, even though that was years before I joined the LIA. I think he's gone around the bend." He made the ancient sign for crazy.

"He was my contact—he was supposed to connect me with Betzy. But he picked you instead and orchestrated the Milo's handoff. Maybe he thought you would be a good way to get in with Marjatta."

"But you said he didn't know Marjatta was important." I poured more coffee but left it sitting in my cup.

"That part isn't completely clear yet. I really think he's a bit off his rocker—maybe he didn't realize you were with Lady Lipinski yesterday. Anyway, he had his goons grab you two last night. I got Marjatta's cell unlocked, then I came for you."

He'd rescued Marjatta first. My stupid heart dove into my shoes again. I knew he wasn't in love with me—why couldn't my heart and brain get onto the same page?

"I knew she could get us out if I didn't manage to free you. I found you, we escaped, Marjatta saved the day." He fiddled with his spoon, not meeting my eyes.

I waited, but he didn't go on. "Now what? Where is Warenton? Is it safe for me to go back to Luna City?" My chest contracted. Not only was Nick not in love with me, but I might lose my home, my job, and my best friend. Where would I go? Would I have to live in the tunnels with Mother Frane? A cold trickle went down my spine.

"I think you'll be fine. Marjatta will take care of you."

"Does she know you're a double agent?"

His blond hair sparkled in the faux sunlight as he shook his head.

I clutched the tablecloth, my voice low and trembling. "What does this make me? I don't want to be a traitor."

His head snapped up, his eyes meeting mine. "You aren't a traitor. You're trying to find a better life for Lunites—and Leweians. That's what the LFF does. We can use someone like you."

I pushed back my chair and turned away, so he wouldn't see my expression. The truth was, I didn't care what the LFF wanted or what the LIA thought. All I cared about was what Nick Beckett wanted. And I wanted it to be me.

I took a deep breath and pushed it out. Then I swung around and pointed a finger at him. "You said no more lies. What's your real name?"

EPISODE 34: NO TIME TO THINK UP NEW LIES

NICK BLINKED AT ME, as if I'd just grown a second head. "What?"

"What's your real name? I'm deciding whether to trust you—and I need to know who you really are."

He bit his lip, and his eyes darted away.

"No—no time to think up new lies. What's your name?"

"It really is Nick. Nicholas Andre. And Beckett is a family name."

"But not your real name." It wasn't a question.

His head shook. "No. I can't tell you my real last name. That would be dangerous—for both of us. But I still need your help. If you're willing."

I crossed my arms and stared out the fake window at the view of Lewei City. One of the many places I wanted to visit someday. Nick said he could help me travel. I could walk away and mourn the fact that Nick wasn't in love with me and probably never would be. Or I could build a wall around my heart and play his game. Decision made, I turned back to him. "I want to go there." I pointed at the window.

"Lewei City? Only the really wealthy get this view. I think this is a feed from the penthouse of the Zhengzu-Maryought. Normal people live pretty much like anyone on Luna City."

I spread my arms. "Normal people don't stay in the Seasons in Paris, either. Yet here I am. I'll keep helping you if you can get me there." I point at the window.

"I can't promise the Zhengzu-Maryought, but I can probably get you to Lewei City." He held out his fist.

"Deal." I bumped my knuckles against his. "Hey, you never told me how you found me. You said you lied—what did you mean?"

His lips twitched in a way I was coming to recognize as self-deprecating. "I was hoping you'd forgotten that. Remember how I told you the cufflink was a tracker?"

"You also told me it was a data card. And just a cufflink. What now—is it a secret transporter machine?"

"No, it's still a tracker. But I also slipped one into your food."

"You what?" I stared at the remains of our breakfast.

"Not that meal—Friday night. The food we picked up at Milo's. You swallowed a tracker that allowed me to find you."

I put a hand to my stomach. "Is it still in there? Will it... pass through? Or stay in me forever?"

He tapped his Ncuff. "It's still in there." He tilted the device so I could see the screen, but I ignored it.

"Why did you put a tracker in my food? You knew I was going on the tour! I should have been completely safe!" I swallowed hard, hoping my breakfast would stay in my stomach. Heaving that up wouldn't get the tracker out of me any faster.

"But you weren't. And, incidentally, that wasn't my fault. You're the one who invited Marjatta to join you."

"I didn't invite—" I snapped my mouth shut. I wasn't going to throw Marjatta under the shuttle. "Don't try to weasel your way out of this! You slipped electronics into my dinner!"

"And it saved your life! Remember what I told you? I will always have your back—even if you're running out of air on the lunar plain. But I can't be there with a spare tank and patch kit if I don't know where you are."

"Well, next time, tell me before you do it! I deserve to know if you're tracking me!"

"Fair enough. After all, that's one of the things the LFF is fighting for—freedom from surveillance." He held up one hand, palm out, and put the other over his chest. "From here on out, I promise to check with you first before I plant a tracker on—"

"Or in!"

"—or in you." He grinned, but the smile faded. "You don't know how glad I was that I'd done it. When you didn't come back for the dinner..."

"I blew your cover?"

He moved closer. "You didn't blow my cover. I told them you weren't feeling well—everyone believed it. No, Katie, I—this is stupid. We haven't known each other very long, but when I found you'd been kidnapped by the mob, I—" He broke off.

"What?" I asked softly, putting a hand on his chest.

He looked away. "I shouldn't say this. It's not professional. But I don't think I could live with myself if anything happened to you." He reached out slowly, almost tentatively, settling his hands on my hips. "I think I'm falling in love with you, Katie Li."

I stared up into his beautiful eyes. Was he telling the truth? I didn't really care anymore.

"And now, if you allow, I'm going to kiss you."

"Not if I kiss you first." I leaned forward and pressed my lips to his.

———

"Are you sure he wasn't just…" Marjatta gave me a pitying stare.

"What? You think a guy like Nick couldn't fall for an ordinary girl like me?" It was a few days later, and we sat in Marjatta's room, snacking on healthy protein cookies.

"It's not you—I'm not sure a guy like Nick can fall for anyone." She sipped her tea. "He's an LIA agent. They don't have feelings like normal people."

I smiled to myself. Marjatta didn't know everything about Nick. She didn't know he was a double agent, and she didn't know how he felt about me. "I'm not worried. We belong together."

She patted my hand. "I hope you're right. But I'm here for you, if you need me. When does he come back to Luna?"

"I'm not sure. He'll let me know."

Her eyes narrowed, and her teacup hit the saucer with a loud clink. "That doesn't sound very good. Men who are in love aren't cagey about when they'll see you again."

"You said it yourself—he's not a normal guy. But I didn't say we wouldn't see each other. I said I didn't know when he'd be back to Luna."

She leaned forward and grabbed my hand. "What's that supposed to mean?"

I lifted a shoulder in a nonchalant shrug. "Just that I'm going to visit him on Lewei next month."

"What? How'd you manage that?"

"I applied for a visa and put in a request for time off. LCL owes me about three weeks of vacation time. And the Leweian government has no reason to turn me down." In fact, Nick would make sure my visa was approved. He needed me on Lewei for a mission.

But more importantly, he needed me.

———

If you enjoyed this story, the Phoenix and Katie Li return in the next *Tales of a Former Space Janitor: Waxing the Moon of Lewei*.

ACKNOWLEDGMENTS

DECEMBER 2021

As I mentioned at the beginning, this story was originally written as a serial. In fact, the first twenty-six episodes were posted online as they were written. And since I don't plot my stories in advance, that was both liberating and a little terrifying. What if I discovered something I'd written in episode five was incompatible with later bits? To make it even crazier, I wrote *Waxing the Moon of Lewei* in between writing these episodes, even though it happens later in the timeline. And since Katie and Nick play a role in that story, I had to make sure this one ended in a way that lead into *Waxing*--which I finished first! But I seem to have an an army of plotters hiding in my subconscious, and they didn't let me down.

The story is set up to allow me to write another "season" to follow this one. By the time you read this, I may have already started working on that. It depends on what my serial readers say. I may choose to write the second season as a book and skip the serialization. I'm completely up in the air on this right now! If you enjoyed the story, let me know what you think. Shoot me a note at: julia@juliahuni.com

While you're at it, if you go to my webpage, you can sign up to get news on my latest releases, some free stories, and other goodies.

––––––

As always, there are lots of folks to thank. First of all, thanks to my husband who gives me the time, space, and support to write. And for being my first serial reader, even when I told him I'd give him the finished manuscript instead. And for creating a beautiful book cover.

I'd like to thank my Kickstarter backers. I launched the "Gooey Galactic Center" campaign to fund the audio book for *Glitter in the Stars (Space Janitor Three)* and this book was one of the rewards for that campaign. So thank you, kind backers! Their names will live on in history--right here and in *Waxing the*

Moon of Lewei. Their support has been unstinting! Special thanks to Rosheen, my fabulous first Patreon supporter.

This book would not have been nearly as good without my editor, Paula Lester of Polaris Editing. Any mistakes you find I undoubtedly added after she finished polishing the manuscript. Thanks to my beta readers, Anne Kavcic, Barb Collishaw, and Jenny Avery, for finding the errors that hid in the dark.

Thanks to my sprint group, Hillary, Paula, AM, Kate, Marcus, Tony, and Lou, for keeping me working even when I'd rather be eating cheesecake. Or baking it. And, of course, thanks to the Big Guy who makes all things possible.

My Fabulous Kickstarter Backers:
Adva Shaviv
Angelica Quiggle
AnnaMarie Enerson
Anne K.
Annie Jenkins
Anonymous Reader
Barb Collishaw
Becky Willis
Brent Held
Bridget Horn
CAP
Charles Rich
Chris Patterson
Chrissy Chronert
Damian Mullins
Dara Girard
Don Bartenstein
Donivan Patwell
Donna Meraz
Duane
Edward C Smith
Emma Allen-Goss
Eva Holmquist
F.A. Hakimian
Gary Olsen
Grace Ela Miah Jack Sarah
Howard Yamaguchi
Ian Bannon
James Vink
Jane
Jane Bond

Jen L
Jennifer Vayhinger
Jim Gotaas
John Jutoy
John Lagerquist
John Prigent
Jon Buller
Just Jeff
Kari Kilgore
Karl Hakimian
Katherine Gordon
Kathy
Kelli King
Krystal Bohannan
Lauren
Lawrence M. Schoen
Liliana Espinoza
Lucas D.
Lydia T.
Marc Sangalli
Marian Goldeen
Meredith Selvoski
Mike Hall
Moe Naguib
None
Norm Coots
Patrick Dempsey
Paul Godtland
Paul Parker
Paul Winfield
Paul Wright
R.S. Kellogg
Regina D.
rlparker
Rob Crosby
Rosheen
Ross Bernheim
S Busby
Sam B.
Sandy Anderson
Sarah Heile
Sheryl Knowles

Stephen Ballentine
Steven Bolbot
Steven Whysong
Sue Laing
Ted Klosowski
Ted M. Young
Thomas Bull
Thomas Cook
Tim Greenshields
Your old pal, Marcus

ALSO BY JULIA HUNI

Colonial Explorer Corps Series:

The Earth Concurrence

The Grissom Contention

The Saha Declination

Colonial Explorer Corps (books 1-3)

Recycled World Series:

Recycled World

Reduced World

Space Janitor Series:

The Vacuum of Space

The Dust of Kaku

The Trouble with Tinsel

Orbital Operations

Glitter in the Stars

Sweeping S'Ride

Triana Moore, Space Janitor (the complete series)

Tales of a Former Space Janitor:

The Rings of Grissom

Planetary Spin Cycle

Waxing the Moon of Lewei

The Phoenix and Katie Li:

Luna City Limited

Krimson Empire (with Craig Martelle)**:**

Krimson Run

Krimson Spark

Krimson Surge

Krimson Flare

Krimson Empire (the complete series)